Toil and Trouble

MODERN MAGICK, 2

CHARLOTTE E. ENGLISH

1

GUESS WHO WAS LANDED with the job of looking after the foul-mouthed book?

'Get this horrid thing out of my library!' said Val. It was an order, but she looked at me in a desperate, pleading way which, as her friend, I could not ignore. 'Ves!'

'Something must certainly be done about it,' I agreed, though my mind was blank as to what, exactly, one could do with an unusually lively sixteenth-century tome with all the tender sensibility of a guttersnipe.

'Base, beetle-headed fool!' raged the book, hovering still before poor Valerie's face. 'Thou hast cracked my spine!'

'Beetle-headed?' whispered Jay to me. 'Now it's just making them up.'

'I have not!' protested Val, and truly, I could hardly think of a more vicious insult to direct at our head librarian.

She'd probably die before she would handle an old book so carelessly as to damage it. 'But I will, if you don't stop,' she added, and I blinked, shocked.

'*Cracked*,' repeated the book. 'Next thou shalt bend thyself to the creasing of my pages! To the turning of my very corners, and the pinching of them, until, full broken, they have not the means of righting themselves!'

'I suppose "dog-eared" must be a recently coined term,' reflected Jay, watching the book with the dispassionate, arms-folded stance of an intrigued scholar.

'I like his version,' I protested. 'Verbose, elegant, poetic—'

'Windy, flowery and over the top.'

I had long suspected that Jay lacked something in the way of soul. Here was complete proof.

'*Jay!*' thundered Valerie, making both of us jump. Admittedly, she did have to raise her voice considerably in order to be heard over the abominable book, which ranted on and on, unabashed. 'This is your doing, and you will fix it at once!'

'Mine?' gasped Jay. 'How is it my fault?!'

'You brought it here!'

'Together with several other works of great historical interest, all of which are far better-behaved,' I reminded her.

'Yes,' said Valerie, and smiled. 'Thank you for those, Jay.'

'You're welcome.'

'But *get rid of this one!*'

Jay looked not only reluctant to saddle himself with such an object (and who could blame him), but also at a loss as to what to do with it if he did. It was only about his third or fourth week with the Society, after all, and this was a species of magickal heritage that even the veterans amongst us had never seen or heard of before (most assuredly including yours truly). So I hastily stepped forward and, feeling heroic and martyred, swept up the book.

'Thank you, Ves,' said Valerie, instantly mollified.

I only sighed. 'May I ask how it came to start talking? For it was as silent as any a book should be, all the way here from Farringale.'

'I opened it.'

'That's it?'

'That's it. It started shrieking blue murder at once, and I did not even get to read any of it because the vile thing kept slamming itself upon my fingers.'

'A deserved torment, craven wench,' the book informed her.

Valerie cast it a look of intense dislike. 'Sorry to land you with that, Ves,' she said. 'But I can't have it in the library all day. It's making far too much noise.'

She was right, of course. We were only in the library's entrance hall, in fact, where Val's grand desk stood; the

3

library itself was through a handsome archway a few feet to my left, whereupon it stretched away and away for some distance. Nonetheless, I had no doubt that the book's ringing tones could be heard all the way at the bottom of the library, which would be pleasing the Society's scholars to no end.

'I don't suppose you have any suggestions...?' I ventured, feeling almost as much at a loss as Jay.

Valerie massaged her temples. There were deep shadows under her dark eyes, and I wondered how long she'd been grappling with the book before we'd finally arrived. 'I don't know exactly, but there's no doubt this is one of our weirder acquisitions. A curse, or a haunting? You might try Zareen.'

'Oh, yes,' I said. 'This is right up her alley.'

'Good luck.' She gave me a grim smile, which I just about managed to return.

Away went Jay and I.

ORDINARILY, JAY IS MUCH better at finding his way around than me, and I am forced to follow him about like a trusting little lamb while he marches us off to wherever we're going. But not at Home. It's a huge, sprawling old place, and while it was built in the sixteen-hundreds it's had all kinds of additions, alterations and expansions made in the centuries since. Having spent more than a decade wandering its winding passages, I know it extremely well.

Thus I was able to sweep out of the library, chin high, and strut confidently away, with Jay trailing meekly along behind me. Felt good. I waited for Jay's inevitable complaint — on the topic of Zareen, most likely, towards whom he has reportedly developed an instant (and mutual) antipathy — but he was silent.

So was the book.

This surprised me so much that I stopped walking, having travelled only about twenty paces down the tapestried corridor. 'Hello?' I said, tentatively.

'To whom do you speak?' said the book, after a moment's pause.

'Why, to you.'

'Well met, lady.'

'How polite. I had rather expected curses.'

'Thou hast not merited such treatment.'

Jay said, 'Better not open it.'

I had to agree. Cradling the book carefully, I ventured on, and Jay fell in beside me. We had not far to go. The structure at Home is as chaotic in the organisational sense as in the geographical; we are loosely separated into divisions, but there is so much bleed-over between the daily duties, challenges and obstacles faced by our various groups that the structure often falls down. Jay and I, for example, are officially part of Acquisitions, but I'm periodically seconded into Research (happy days, those), and I wouldn't be at all surprised if Jay ends up handed off to Zareen's division more often than he's going to like.

Technically, Zareen is part of Research, albeit in an unusual capacity. But she consults for Development from time to time, and I bump into her in Acquisitions here and there, too. She runs an obscure little division almost single-handedly, clumsily shelved under Research because nobody knows what else to call it. And since it has never been given its own, official name, we've collectively dubbed it the Toil and Trouble division.

In other words: when anything particularly weird comes up, we all call in Zareen.

She's usually holed up not far from the library, in a tiny nook of a room buried deep in the west wing. The door is always shut.

'Would you mind knocking?' I said to Jay once we had arrived. 'I don't want to risk dropping the book.'

'Perish the thought.' Jay shuddered, and knocked smartly upon the door. He then adopted a pose of such studied nonchalance as clearly displayed his discomfort, and I tried my best not to notice.

'Hang on a minute!' yelled Zareen. There came some clattering noises from the other side of the door, and we were left to enjoy the chill of the dim, stone-walled corridor (bare of tapestries, paintings or anything else in this part of the House) for half a minute longer.

Then the door swung open, apparently by itself, revealing Zareen seated at a desk tucked into the corner of the room. The place was a mess, as usual; books and notepads were stacked everywhere, along with a host of such peculiar paraphernalia I'd have no idea where to begin in describing it. Case in point, though: a collection of skulls, apparently human, sat clustered at one end of her desk, except that they were palm-sized, and as usual she had an odd contraption made of woven string, jewel-charms and bones hung upon the wall above her chair. Her curse-catcher, she calls it. I've never been able to figure out whether its purpose is merely decorative, or functional — and if the latter, what its function is supposed to be.

The lady herself looked me over with considerable goodwill, and then Jay with rather less. She had green streaks in her black hair today, very neatly done, and she sported a matching green jewel in her nose ring.

'Peridot?' I enquired.

'It's new.' Zareen grinned and swung around to face me, giving me a full view of the new jewellery.

'Suits you.'

'Doesn't it?' Zareen turned her amused gaze upon Jay, who bore it rigidly. 'I'm still working on Ves. What do you think, nostril or septum?'

'I've told you,' I said hastily. 'I'll think about it when you find me a good unicorn stud, and not before.'

'You can't wear a unicorn in your nose. Pick something smaller.'

'I can't? Then I'm not getting my nose pierced.'

'Navel maybe,' murmured Zareen, but she was watching Jay.

'Do the women of this miserable age commonly engage in bodily mutilation?'

It was the book speaking, of course, but since I had yet to warn Zareen of its capacity to do so, she narrowed her eyes at the only male in the room: Jay.

'That was not me!' he protested. 'Did you see my mouth move?'

'Just the kind of prissy thing you would say,' retorted Zareen, ignoring his question.

I headed off what was clearly an impending fight by laying the book in front of Zareen. I'd been clutching it to my chest until then, with my arms wrapped tightly around it, and since she was used to seeing me carting books everywhere (who wasn't, indeed?) I don't suppose it had occurred to her to take note of it. But the book got her attention at once, as I'd known it would, for on the front of its dark leather cover there was engraved a motif of a complex star, a flame blossoming at each of its twelve points.

'Ooh,' said Zareen, captivated.

'Don't open it yet,' I warned.

She was itching to do so, already reaching for it. 'What?'

I explained.

Zareen was not impressed.

'You've brought me a centuries-old book from *Farringale*,' she said with emphasis. 'A book no one's read since the sixteen-hundreds, containing who knows what esoteric wisdom, and I can't open it?'

'Well, you can,' I allowed. 'Only get some ear plugs first, maybe.'

'And watch your fingers,' put in Jay.

Zareen scowled at him. 'I've handled difficult artefacts before.'

Jay rolled his eyes. 'By all means, try it.'

Zareen did, though to her credit she looked a little wary, and opened it with a hesitancy unusual for her.

'Fool-born haggard!' erupted the book, right on cue. 'Dost thou *dare* to venture upon mine innards? Thou wouldst disembowel me of all my goodness, wouldst thou, and with narry a *by-your-leave!*' The book slammed shut with a crisp *snap* of disapproval.

'Ow,' said Zareen, shaking the pain out of her fingertips.

Jay, wisely, refrained from airing the *I-told-you-so* I could see hovering upon his lips. Instead he said, 'We're calling him Bill.'

'As in Shakespeare?'

'Quite.'

'Slightly less elegantly verbose, I'd say?'

'His full name is Bill the Boor.'

'Churl,' said the book.

'Boor,' said Jay.

'So,' I said brightly. 'Bit of a problem, no? Val would've skinned me alive if I hadn't taken it away at once, and I'm afraid nobody could think who could possibly fix it but you.'

Alone among those who had come into contact with the wretched book, Zareen looked intrigued — even a little bit excited. 'Nice,' she murmured, and turned the book around on her desk, examining all the features of its covers and spine. She ignored its ongoing diatribe with admirable grace.

'Curse or haunting, do you think?' I asked, remembering Val's words.

'Could be either! Really interesting stuff.'

'I can't tell you how glad we are that you think so.' I had no hesitation in speaking for Jay as well as myself, for I could see the relief on his face. Tinged, maybe, with a hint of fascinated disgust.

Well, it takes most people a little while to get used to Zareen.

She was barely listening, already absorbed in the many questions posed by the book. 'Thanks, Ves,' she said vaguely. 'I'll call you when I've figured it out.'

What bliss it was to walk out of that room, and close the door behind us! We walked quickly away, pursued by the muffled and increasingly distant sounds of sixteenth-century cursing.

'She's got a strong stomach,' I offered.

'Madwoman,' he replied, though he didn't sound as negative as I'd expected. Perhaps Zareen had actually won herself a few points with Jay for her willingness to take the thing off our hands.

'Cup of tea?' said I.

'*Yes.*'

2

In my room at Home, I've got a little stash of Curiosities, minor artefacts, and assorted odds and ends. Some of them are useful, some of them aren't. Probably my favourite of the latter category is a beautiful old scroll, the real kind, made of vellum and with rowan-wood supports. It even has a tooled-leather case. It's paired with a quill pen — owl feather, not goose! Both are enchanted, so that anything I might choose to write upon mine will appear at once upon the matching scrolls of some other member (or members) of the Society. They used to be standard issue, but they stopped handing them out before I joined. I once found a whole, sorry stack of them in Stores, and took pity on this set because... because they're pretty.

What can I say.

The reason for their obsolescence, of course, is the mobile phone. When we all wander about with smartphones surgically attached to our wrists, who needs quills and scrolls anymore? A sad casualty of cruel, inexorable time.

But, I have to admit, a fair one. For when, a few hours later, my own personal scroll-killer buzzed and began to play *Sussudio,* it got my attention at once, and within two minutes I was rattling back down to Research and Zareen's broom-cupboard of a room.

Zareen opened the door right away. 'You're going to like this,' she said, grinning and ushering me inside.

I eyed the book with misgivings. It lay quiescent upon the desk, quiet as a proverbial church mouse, but I didn't trust it. 'I rather doubt that.'

'Oh, don't worry. It's much nicer now.'

'It is? What did you do to it?'

Zareen wouldn't meet my eye. 'Uh, just some minor tweaks. Never mind that. What do you think I found inside?'

'You've read it!'

'Sort of. There isn't much to read, as it turns out. Only a few pages have been used. It looks like a journal, used to record somebody's progress upon some kind of journey. Late Middle English, I'd say, so it's hard to read, and written in such deplorable chicken-scratch I can hardly make it out. So the destination's unclear — or at least, it was at *first.*'

Zareen was bursting with news, and very smug about it too. I didn't want to stop her, but I had to ask: 'Wait, where's Jay?'

'No idea. Anyway, the—'

'Stop right there.' I grabbed my phone and called Jay, ignoring Zareen's eye-rolling disgust. 'Toil and Trouble,' I told Jay when he answered. 'All due haste.'

'Be right there.'

I put my phone away. 'It's Jay's book,' I said. 'And I'm his... mentor, I suppose. Can't leave him out.'

Zareen waited with an exaggerated display of patience.

'What's the problem with you two, anyway?'

'Oh, nothing really,' Zareen replied with a roll of her eyes. 'I think he's a prude and a stick-in-the-mud and he thinks I'm reckless and irresponsible.' She gave me a half-smile. 'Just squabbles, Ves. Don't worry about it.'

Me, worry? I wanted to disclaim this charge at once, until I realised I was wearing my worried face. I hastily smoothed out my features and adopted an air of proper unconcern. 'I feel responsible for him,' I said by way of explanation.

'I don't think you need to be. I'll say this for him: he's far from stupid, and he'll always be okay.'

'Mm.'

Zareen looked at me shrewdly. 'He feels responsible for you, too, I think.'

'Me!'

Zareen grinned. 'Surprised? He *was* given the job of making sure we don't lose you somewhere.'

'Making sure I don't lose myself somewhere, you mean? Fair.'

'No easy task.'

I couldn't argue with this judgement, since it was true. Thankfully for my dignity, Jay showed up just then. He was polite enough to greet Zareen with a nod, and looked at me. 'What's the news?'

'Your moment's arrived,' I said to Zareen. 'We're ready to be impressed!'

Zareen leaned back in her chair, put her booted feet up on her desk and said, 'It's a treasure map.'

'What?' said Jay. 'Bill?'

'Sort of. The book, as I've just said to Ves, contains a somewhat wandering and confused account of somebody's journey in search of something unidentified, to places unspecified. Not at all edifying, and so poorly written I can't even decipher most of it. Only the first few pages have been written on, and one page at the back, which contains a sketch.'

'A map!' I said.

Zareen nodded, grinning. 'It's got an X-marks-the-spot and everything.' She displayed for us a piece of notepaper, upon which she had apparently copied the map in red pen. Her X in the middle was huge and exuberant, marked in bold.

'How do we know it's a treasure map?' said Jay, prosaically.

I sighed. 'Ancient maps with an X marked somewhere upon them are always treasure maps.'

Zareen nodded. 'That, and there's an obscure reference on the third page to a bounty of some kind, if I'm reading it right. There's no description as to what manner of treasure the writer was after, but he obviously expected to discover some grand prize.'

'Any idea as to the identity of the writer?' I asked.

'None.'

'Did you ask Bill?' said Jay.

'I tried. He wouldn't stop insulting me long enough to answer my questions.'

Jay and I both looked in silence at the book. It hadn't spoken a word since I'd entered the room, fully quarter of an hour before. 'I'm curious,' said Jay. 'How did you shut it up?'

Zareen shifted in her seat, and avoided Jay's eye. And mine. 'Er, I haven't. He's just a bit less noisy now.'

I considered pressing the matter — Zareen was obviously skirting around the edges of something — but on reflection I let it pass. Sometimes it's best to circle around the point. So I said: 'What's the likelihood that Bill, or wherever that voice is coming from, is the same person who wrote the journal entries and sketched the map?'

'You mean, is this a haunting? I don't think so. When he wasn't insulting me, he was protesting against the very idea that he'd write such uncouth nonsense, or hare around searching for treasure just because somebody drew a map. Whatever became of the writer, I don't think it's Bill. And I'm not convinced that the book's haunted by anybody else, either, for he's showed no signs of having any kind of history that he can remember, and ghosts can usually talk about little else. You'll want to interrogate him a bit more yourself, see if you can't get more out of him.'

I reached for the book.

'Later,' added Zareen hastily.

I sat back again. 'So it's not a haunting. A curse, then?'

'Could be, but it's the oddest curse I've ever come across if so. Yes, he was keeping idle hands from opening the book and thereby keeping anybody from reading it, but it's a clumsy form of protection. It didn't take much to get around that problem.'

'Oh?'

Zareen indicated a pair of heavy marble paperweights upon her desk. 'It took a few tries, but I peaced it and put weights upon its pages. Bill went off for a nice little nap, and when he woke up it was too late to take up snapping at my fingers again.' She paused and added reflectively, 'He took it rather well, all things considered, which again leads me to think that he isn't there to deter people from reading it. He's just a bad-tempered grouch.'

'But if he's not a ghost or a curse, what is he?'

'A spell,' said Zareen with a shrug. 'Though I grant you, it's a sophisticated enchantment, and more complex than anything I've ever met with before. Quite intimidating. But considering where you got the thing, I shouldn't be surprised.'

I took it from this that Zareen had no more idea what the spell was intended to accomplish than I did. And how intriguing a puzzle. A complicated enchantment which had gifted an (apparently) ordinary book with sentience — and an extraordinarily foul vocabulary? One which had, considering the nature of that vocabulary, been placed upon the book some four or five hundred years ago? And one which, for all its sophistication, Zareen had managed to get around with quite a simple charm?

Very curious indeed.

'If someone was going to go to all that trouble,' said Jay, 'I wonder why they didn't make it more... polite.'

I couldn't help but be tickled by the idea. 'That's a sense of humour I can appreciate.'

Jay grinned. 'It doesn't quite fit with the legends of old Farringale, though, does it? The royal court, a place of learning and high art, blah blah.'

'You'd expect it to express itself in the courtliest language, and with perfect etiquette.'

Zareen looked shifty again. 'Er, yes. You would.'

'So the map,' said Jay, and leaned over the book to get a closer look at it. 'Where does it lead to?'

Zareen pushed her sketch nearer. 'Might want to consult Val. There's only one word on it, and when I did a search I didn't get any hits.'

'*Drogryre,*' read Jay.

'No hits at all?' I repeated, incredulous.

'Not one. So this place is—'

'—even more lost to the mists of time than Farringale,' I finished.

'Or just an extremely well-kept secret,' suggested Jay. He picked up the map and stuck it in his pocket, then made to collect the book, too.

Zareen stopped him. 'Where are you going with those?'

'To find Drogryre. Isn't that what we do next?'

'Let Ves take the book.'

This requirement made as much sense to me as it did to Jay, who looked irritated. But he complied, stepping back to make room for me.

I picked up the book very carefully, still expecting it to hurl abuse at me. But it remained blissfully quiet.

'Don't open it until you get to the library,' Zareen recommended.

'Why not?' I said.

'It's asleep right now.'

'What do you mean by—' I began, but the door was already closing behind us.

'Bring me back something with bones!' yelled Zareen through the door as we walked away.

'There's something fishy about all that,' said Jay.

I had to agree. We made it halfway back to the library before curiosity overcame the both of us. 'I have to open it,' I said.

'Go on,' said Jay.

We stopped in an alcove beneath a big, bright window and I took hold of the front cover. 'Here we go.'

To my relief, the book suffered itself to be opened without trying to bite my fingers, and without snapping itself shut again. Nor did it drown me in a barrage of abuse.

But it did speak.

'Madam,' said the book. 'You must allow me to tell you how ardently I admire and love you.'

I slammed the book shut.

Silence.

Then Jay said, in a strangled voice, 'Is Bill quoting Pride and Prejudice?'

'Dear Jay,' I said faintly. 'I could not be more impressed with your familiarity with the utterances of Mr. Darcy, I assure you.'

'Why is it coming out of *this* book?' said Jay, ignoring my implied question with superb grace.

Gingerly, I opened it up again. And there, on the first unused page, was the whole of Mr. Darcy's ill-fated proposal to Elizabeth Bennet, written out in Zareen's rounded handwriting.

'Val,' I said slowly, 'is going to kill all of us.'

'Probably with a dessert spoon.'

3

ALL THINGS CONSIDERED, JAY and I made an executive decision not to take the book straight back to Val. We carried it instead to my favourite study carrell, which happened to be safely situated two large rooms and a corridor away from the library.

It was pleasant to tuck back up in there again. It's a modest place — just a desk (albeit a splendidly well-preserved nineteenth-century example, all mahogany and mother-of-pearl), and a chair (ditto), placed in a concealed alcove off one of the reference rooms. I've spent untold hours there with stacks and stacks of books, researching one obscure topic after another. It's undoubtedly *my* study nook.

Jay took to it at once, for I caught him glancing around with an admiring, speculative look.

'Mine,' I told him.

'Sorry.'

I put the book carefully down upon the desk and — checking first to make sure nobody was too near to us — I opened it again.

'Good morning, madam,' said the book. 'Good morning, sir.'

'You can call me Jay,' said Jay.

'That would be an improper mode of address, sir, particularly in view of the fact that we have not yet been introduced.'

I summoned my best manners, and formally introduced Jay to the book. Jay made a decidedly courtly bow, which impressed me no end.

Then he introduced me, and I felt it incumbent upon me to match his exquisite etiquette with a curtsey.

It was an odd business.

The book was kind enough to overlook the irregularities in our behaviour, mostly because, as he said himself: 'I am not fortunate enough to have a large acquaintance here. In fact, I know no one else except for the odd, vulgar woman with the green hair, whose identity remains a mystery.'

Jay stifled his laughter — barely. 'You have no objection to Ves's pink hair?'

'The arrangement of Miss Vesper's hair might be highly irregular, but there is nothing to fault in her manners.'

I was glad he'd said that, for I was quite attached to my hair colour of the day. Rose pink (the dusky, antique shade), and perfectly curled. 'Thank you, Bill,' I said, beaming.

'We can't call him Bill anymore,' said Jay.

'An unnecessarily abbreviated name,' agreed the book.

'We can still call him Bill,' I offered. 'Darcy's first name was Fitzwilliam.'

'Bill Darcy it is.'

The book objected, but I overrode him. 'Matters are not as they were when you were written, Bill,' I unhappily had to inform him. 'You had better get used to our unnecessarily abbreviated modes of address.'

'If you insist, Miss Vesper.'

I gave up.

Secretly, I rather enjoyed being called "Miss Vesper." Jay, however, did not take so enthusiastically to "Mr Patel". 'That is my father,' he said sternly. 'Jay, please.'

The book heaved a resigned sigh, and capitulated.

Having got the formalities out of the way, it was time to do as Zareen had suggested, and launch a clever and subtle interrogation of Bill. I began with: 'Where does your map lead, Bill?'

'To the grave of my mistress.'

'Mistress?' said Jay.

'*Grave*?' said I.

Jay began to laugh. 'So much for treasure.'

'I do not at all understand the modern fixation upon "treasure",' said Bill in disgust. 'It was all that green woman would talk of.'

'That's acquisitions specialists for you,' I said by way of apology. 'The hearts of magpies, all of us.'

'To return to my mistress,' said Bill stonily, '*She* was the greatest sorceress of the age, and my noble creator. In this respect, perhaps, she was a far greater treasure than any mere gold.'

This was interesting. 'Go on. Why did she make you?'

'I was to serve as her grimoire, but of a far cleverer design than any that had yet been created. My task was to absorb not only my mistress's knowledge but anything else that should come in my way, and to repeat it upon command.'

'That *is* clever!'

'I believe I did save my mistress a great deal of time and trouble,' said Bill modestly. 'And won for her no small number of esoteric secrets, besides.'

Jay brightened at the word "secrets". So did I. Occupational hazard. 'We,' I said to Bill, 'are going to get along very well, I think.'

'It is my dearest wish that we should, Miss Vesper.'

'He definitely likes *you*,' muttered Jay.

I awarded the book a tender little pat of approval. 'What about the map?' I asked. 'And your first few pages? They were not written by your mistress, clearly.'

Bill bristled with indignation, his pages curling in a bookish grimace. 'Her death was sudden—'

'How did she die?' interpolated Jay.

'A form of plague.'

'My condolences.'

'Thank you. Her death was sudden, and I was lost for some years among a number of other, lesser volumes from her collection. We were lodged for a time in the library of the great house, until one day we were stolen by a deplorable varmint of the name of John Wester. If you have read those pages, madam, then you will have already experienced his disgraceful mode of expressing himself and I need not elaborate.'

'I haven't, yet, but you did give a rather excellent demonstration of them.'

The book looked a trifle sheepish, and shuffled about upon the desk. 'I did not, at first, trouble myself to speak much to Wester. I was delighted to be removed from the dusty shelf upon which I had so long languished, and entertained some hopes of finding my new master congenial. And I was curious as to his reasons, for he took only two books from the house's collection, both from my mistress's former possessions: a slim treatise upon the most ancient and respectable practices of star-magick, of which my mistress was a devotee. And me. But if I hoped that his second choice, at least, indicated that he understood some part of my value, I was to be disappointed. He had noticed only that my pages were apparently blank, and secured me in order to serve as a receptacle for his own records. My dignity was sunk indeed.

'The matter which absorbed all his curiosity was the search for my mistress's grave. He was under the impression that some article of great value had been buried with her. He was, in other words, a treasure-hunter. He had received some hint of the grave's location, but I understood that, by the time in question — some years after her death — its precise situation was no longer known.'

'What kind of thing was buried with her?' I said, greatly intrigued.

'That I never learned from him. I am not convinced that he knew it himself. He was an opportunist and an adventurer, and not at all averse to taking a chance.'

'Grave-robbers and thieves, plagues and dark sorceresses,' said Jay. 'This is getting good.'

'Zareen will be delighted.'

Bill gave a slight, polite cough. 'I have almost finished.'

'My apologies. Do go on.'

'I did not particularly take to John Wester,' Bill continued, unnecessarily. 'Particularly since the free use he made of my early pages seeped into my consciousness, as was inevitable, and my turn of phrase inevitably adapted itself to his. I made rather free use of his more vulgar vocabulary, and abused him with such spirit every time he dared to approach me that he soon gave up the endeavour. To my great satisfaction, he rid himself of me by selling me to that rare form of travelling merchant who understands when he has met with an object of true worth. I was sold for a mere few shillings, which was a source of some embarrassment to me, but since I afterwards was placed, through a series of subsequent trades, into the grand collections at the Court of the Trolls, I was able to recover my dignity in time.'

'And there you stayed for hundreds of years, until Jay rescued you.' I beamed at Jay, who smiled uncertainly back.

'I am appalled to learn that my sojourn there was of such extended duration,' said Bill. 'I believe I must have slept through most of it.'

'Very likely.' I fell into a reverie of reflection for a little while, pondering Bill's extraordinary tale. Some few questions stood out, at the end of my musings. 'Did they know what you were, at Farringale? Did you speak to them?'

'Scarcely at all, madam. I knew my vocabulary and general speech to be most unsuited to a place of such vaunted learning.'

'A pity, perhaps. All your potential has been wasted.'

'Until now, Miss Vesper. I have some hopes of enjoying a second spring of activity.'

'What became of John Wester, I wonder?' said Jay. 'Did he ever find the grave?'

'And was there anything of interest in it?' said I. 'Good question. Sadly it seems history has forgotten the answers, though perhaps Val might know something.'

Bill gave his polite cough again. 'I wonder if my apologies might be conveyed to the green woman? I have been disgracefully rude both to her and about her, but it strikes me that, without her interference, I would be still condemned to express myself with all the excessive vulgarity of John Wester's cant.'

'Her name is Zareen—' I began.

'—or Miss Dalir, if you prefer,' Jay put in.

'—and I have no doubt she will forgive you, for she enjoyed the mystery you presented very much indeed.'

'She might be disappointed to learn that you aren't a treasure map, though,' Jay cautioned.

'I doubt it,' I disagreed. 'Given the choice, Zareen would always go for a good disinterring over a treasure hunt.'

Jay looked faintly appalled.

'She always was a trifle macabre that way.' I picked up Bill, cradling him in my arms — I was growing rather fond of him by then, I admit — and squared my shoulders. 'No help for it. It's time to see Val. But we've such a fine story to tell that I hope she won't disembowel us *too* badly.'

'Disembowelling is pretty absolute,' Jay said. 'You either lose your entrails or you don't.'

'I'm hoping Bill can be relied upon to present his side of the story with such style as to spare us that fate.'

'I shall be happy to, madam,' said Bill, slightly muffled.

It occurred to me to be grateful even for John Wester's highly questionable behaviour. If he had not stolen Bill back in the sixteenth century, then the book may never have ended up at Farringale, and he would never have come to us. Even if he had, without Wester's journalising the book would have retained his original turn of phrase, which I imagined to be extremely civilised — in a Chaucerian kind of way. Middle English is not precisely my strong point.

'You're quite wonderful, Bill,' I said with fervour.

'Thank you, madam.'

'IT'S AN UNUSUAL NAME,' said Valerie some half an hour later, poring over Zareen's sketch of the map and the single word that adorned it. 'I can't even decide how to pronounce it.'

'Medieval,' said Jay, as though this was both explanation and apology enough.

Val apparently agreed, for she merely nodded.

Our initial half-hour in the library *had* been a bit sticky. While Val was relieved to find our Bill so tidily reformed, she was every bit as horrified by the manner of its accomplishment as I had feared.

'*Ten* years in the dungeons!' she hissed, and began searching through her desk drawers for her phone.

'The House has dungeons?' Jay repeated, awed.

'Excellent ones,' I said. 'They're only cellars really, but "dungeon" sounds much more impressive. And there *are* signs with one or two of them that they might have been built to serve as dungeons in the first place. One of them even has something of the oubliette about it, which is fascinating considering—'

'You're babbling, Ves,' said Jay.

I was. 'Sorry,' I babbled. 'Val, don't murder Zareen. She did us a favour.'

'I'm not going to murder her, I'm going to throw her in the oubliette.'

'She'll love that.'

Val looked uncertain, and stopped searching for her phone. 'She will, won't she? I'll have to think of something else.'

'Disembowelment,' suggested Jay helpfully.

Val's face set into steely lines, and her dark eyes glittered. 'With a spoon.'

'What did I tell you?' I said. 'Stop helping, Jay.'

'Sorry.'

'Listen,' I commanded, and put Bill down upon the desk. 'Tell her, Bill.'

'I am in Miss Dalir's debt,' said Bill obligingly. 'Her methods may have been invasive and uncouth, but the results are so much to my taste that I cannot long hold her coarseness against her.'

Overwhelmed by this display of generosity mixed with disdain, and all couched in such elegant terms, Val could only blink at the book in amazement. 'He really *is* re-formed,' she said.

'Oh, completely,' said Jay. 'He delivers his insults in such stately style, now.'

'He's a refined, sophisticated book,' I objected, 'and did not enjoy turning the air blue any more than we enjoyed hearing it.'

Val gave me an odd look.

'He admires and loves Ves,' said Jay. 'Ardently.'

'Apparently it's mutual.' Val's eyebrows went up.

I coughed.

So did Bill.

'Anyway,' I said brightly. 'Bill's creator?'

'I'll see what I can come up with,' Val promised.

'The name doesn't ring any bells?'

'Not quite.'

I wasn't sure what "not quite" meant in this context, but it sounded more promising than "none whatsoever." So I scooped up Jay — not Bill, unfortunately, for Val claimed him for research purposes — and whisked him off. 'It's high time we reported to Milady.'

'The gruelling climb,' Jay groaned.

'It's good for your health.'

'Tell that to my knees when I'm ninety-five.'

I pictured Jay at ninety-five, wizened and white-haired and still grumbling about the stairs. I had to laugh.

'Your sympathy is touching,' said Jay. We had by that time arrived at the first of the several flights of stairs — stone-cut, narrow and winding, naturally — that led up to Milady's aerie tower, and I laughed even harder as Jay visibly braced himself.

I did not really suspect him of deliberately hamming it up. Not until I noticed a secret half-smile just vanishing from his face as he marched away from me, moving upwards at a smart pace.

'You're teasing me,' I said with strong disapproval, and made sure to overtake him at once.

It was Jay's turn to laugh.

4

'Good morning Vesper, Jay,' said Milady as she admitted us to her room. The air sparkled as her disembodied voice spoke.

'Milady.' I took up my usual station in the centre of the sumptuous blue carpet, and made her a curtsey. Jay produced the same courtly bow he'd offered to Bill earlier.

'Very fine form, Jay,' Milady complimented him.

Jay grinned. 'Thank you.'

'He's been practicing,' I said.

'He will make a fine ambassador to the Courts someday.'

That shut me up. Jay! The Society's representative at the magickal royal courts! Since I'd secretly coveted such posts for some years, I could not help feeling a twinge of envy at the idea.

'Not before you, Ves,' said Jay, apparently reading my feelings. It was so kindly said that I instantly forgave him for his earlier teasing.

'Have you ambassadorial ambitions, Ves?' said Milady.

I sighed. 'I'm a little susceptible to the glamour of the post, I can't deny it. But while I think I would suit such a post well, I would probably grow bored after a while.'

'You would, in fact,' said Jay, though whether he was referring to my assertion of being well-suited to such a job, or to my conviction that it would eventually bore me, I could not determine.

'Very well, I shall not rush to reassign you. And we cannot yet spare Jay from Acquisitions, either. What can you tell me about that terrible book?'

We told her everything about the terrible book. I personally chose to gloss over the close relationship I was beginning to enjoy with dear old Bill, but Jay had no such scruples.

Milady seemed more struck with the book's history than its present configuration. 'I am astounded,' said she when we had finished, 'that this sorceress should have faded so completely from all memory or record, considering the extent of her accomplishments. Such a book must qualify as a great artefact. In fact, I have rarely heard of so spectacular an achievement in magick. Valerie had nothing to tell you?'

'I got the impression she had some kind of an idea,' I replied. 'But too shaky an inkling to share, just yet. I've hopes of hearing something more concrete from her before long.'

'I am sure she can be relied upon to unearth something,' Milady agreed. 'As to the book...' She trailed off into silence, and Jay and I waited patiently while she thought the matter over. 'I think it had better be kept a secret, for the present,' she finally decided. 'Such a powerful object would be so highly sought after, were it known to exist — even now, we have nothing in magick to equal it! I fear there could be trouble over it.'

'Absolutely, Milady,' I said. 'We won't spread it about.'

'Should be easier to keep a lid on it, now that Bill's calmed down,' added Jay.

'Yes,' said Milady. 'There I must agree with Bill. Zareen's methods are somewhat to be deplored, but they do appear to have done the trick this time.'

'That's why we have Zareen,' I said. 'She does the questionable stuff, so most of us don't have to.'

'Not that it stops you from trying,' muttered Jay.

'Sometimes, the strangest tasks require the most difficult procedures,' Milady gracefully agreed, letting Jay's comment pass. I knew that Zareen was often given leeway on this kind of thing, more so than the rest of us. I had never resented it, because I knew it was part of her job; Toil and

Trouble, indeed. She paid dearly for the privilege of *not* being decapitated for such transgressions as, say, copying famous proposals of marriage into ancient books.

'Do keep me informed,' said Milady. 'In the meantime, Ves, I understand you have some few articles withdrawn from Stores, which might wish to be replaced?'

'Er, yes.' I felt a little shame-faced. I'd gone a bit mad in the store-rooms on the last mission, and gleefully carted off all manner of shiny charms, magickal trinkets and minor artefacts. Most of which I had not even used, and I had indeed forgotten to return some of them.

I do have terrible hoarding tendencies sometimes.

'Jay,' continued Milady serenely. 'Your sister is in the development labs with Orlando. She is feeling overwhelmed, I believe, and would benefit from some family time.'

'Absolutely,' said Jay.

Knowing ourselves to be dismissed, we made our parting obeisances and left the tower, clattering back down the stairs in some relief. I'd half expected Milady to be appalled at the way we'd handled the book, and was pleased to find that we were not in disgrace.

'Your sister's with *Orlando?*' I asked Jay as we wended our way back down. 'How!'

Orlando's the Development Division's star employee, and a typical eccentric. He's an inventor, of sorts; he mixes old magick with new technology in genius-level ways, and he's responsible for some of our best tools (and weapons). He's very secretive. He lives tucked away up in the attics somewhere, and the only people who are regularly allowed to go into his workrooms are his wife, Miranda, and his assistant, Jeremy.

'She's very bright, and very talented,' said Jay with obvious pride. 'They're considering her for Orlando's new assistant.'

'New? What about Jeremy?'

'They think Orlando could do with some more help.'

Perhaps he could, at that. His inventions were so popular with the Society, I could well believe he might have trouble keeping up with the demand. 'You've a very talented family,' I observed.

Jay smiled. 'Indira will be the best of us. She's had a rough time of it lately, though. No sooner did she arrive here than she broke her arm, and now it sounds like she's homesick. I'd better go right away.'

I realised suddenly that I'd seen her already, a week or two before. Our doctor, Rob, had been tending to her. 'How did she break her arm?'

Jay grimaced. 'Fell down some stairs.'

Perhaps that explained a little of Jay's aversion to them. I filed that away. 'Isn't she a bit young to be apprenticing already? Though perhaps Milady was in a hurry to scoop her up.'

'Yes, and yes,' Jay admitted. 'Though she's older than she looks. She's almost eighteen.'

I'd thought she looked fifteen at most. I felt a surge of sympathy for her, remembering the distressed look on her youthful face when I'd seen her in the infirmary. 'That way to Orlando's secret attic hideaway,' I said a few moments later, pointing down a dark passageway that led away from the second set of stairs. 'He won't let you in, but hopefully he'll send Indira out.'

Jay gave me a salute in thanks, and wandered off. I trailed back downstairs alone, feeling oddly forlorn. Perhaps it was because I had to give up the remains of my hoard to the Stores again. I *do* so like my trinkets.

I wondered, on the way back to my room, how Bill was getting along with Val.

Swimmingly, I found. When I'd finished guiltily gathering up my temporary acquisitions and conveying them back to Stores, I trawled back to the library to find Bill holding court from the centre of Val's desk. His courtiers consisted of the entire library staff — students from research and reference, veterans from the archives, everybody. Val herself sat enthroned in her usual spot, but she looked harassed.

'Madam,' I heard Bill say as I approached. 'You do have the most delightfully smooth fingernails.'

He was addressing Anne from Archives, who blushed to match her fire-red dress and stroked Bill lovingly. 'You're so kind to say so.'

A young man I didn't recognise said: 'What about the curse of Thetford in 1453? Real or hoax?'

'Most likely a hoax,' said Bill firmly. 'The story was fabricated by a linen-weaver called Wymond Bowe, who hated his brother's wife with such a passion that he accused her of sorcery, and claimed that she had cursed the townsfolk with a host of unpleasant ailments. The evidence he presented was certainly spurious, but it is fair to note that the good people of Thetford *did* exhibit an unusually broad range of complaints during that year. There were claims in some quarters that the curse was real (or curses, I should say), and that Bowe was in fact the source of the troubles himself.'

'But you don't believe that.'

Bill considered. 'My mistress was acquainted with Bowe in some distant fashion, and did not give the story much credence.'

'This is brilliant,' said the young man, and immediately began typing furiously into his phone. He snapped Bill's picture.

'Val—' I tried to say, but she could not hear me over the clamour of Bill's audience, and I couldn't get near her either.

But Bill detected my presence, for he cried with alacrity: 'Miss Vesper! Surrounded as I am with extraordinary beauty, still you cast all others into the shade.'

I began to wonder whether our precious book wasn't so much Bill Darcy as Bill Wickham.

I also wondered a bit about Drogryre. Had the book always been so devastatingly charming? (At least up until it came into contact with John Wester).

'Bill,' I said, pushing my way through to the desk with a brutality born of mild desperation. '*Val.* Can we please clear everyone out?'

Val looked relieved to have an excuse. 'All right, back to work!' she shouted. 'There'll be more Bill later.'

Disgruntled, but somewhat mollified by this appended promise, the library's staff drifted away, leaving me alone with Val.

'Milady wants him kept secret,' I hissed.

'It's a bit late for that order.'

'So I see.' I grimaced. 'I ought to have known Bill would cause an instant sensation.'

'He's like a search engine for magickal history, at least up until the sixteenth century. And he's got a vast deal of information that's never come to light before. Of *course* he's a sensation.'

'Not to mention his talent for flattering with sincerity.'

Bill ruffled his pages. 'It may have escaped your attention, madam, but I can hear you.'

I patted Bill's soft leather cover. 'I mean no disparagement, Bill. You're every girl's dream, aren't you?'

Bill appeared pleased with this tribute, and settled down.

'What can we do?' I said, despairing. 'Milady says there'll be trouble if word spreads, and she could well be right. Can you imagine what a book like this would fetch at auction?'

Val began to look worried. 'Spreads where, though? We might receive a few purchase offers, but I can't think who would cause trouble.'

I could think of a few possibilities, but I kept them to myself. It might never happen, and Val had clearly had a trying enough morning already. 'I'm sure it will be fine,' I said. 'Only perhaps we'll keep him under better wraps for a while.'

'We can try,' said Val.

For the rest of the afternoon, I had some of that rare, lovely stuff they call "free time." Jay didn't reappear, and my favourite activity — browsing in Stores — would put me too much in the way of temptation. So instead I spent it on my other favourite activity: browsing in the library.

With Bill. And Val. And half the rest of the Society. My esteemed colleagues kept wandering in all through the afternoon, having *just* happened to remember some vital errand they had to run in the library and which absolutely could not wait another instant... oh, is that the talking book? A quick peek? Bill, do you happen to know the recipe for Gulgorn's Palliative? It's been lost since at least the early fifteens... you do! Let me jot that down! All right, all right, I'm going. Brilliant book you have there.

This went on all day. It was of no use bleating about Milady's orders; our visitors patently did not care, and it was just as obviously too late for us to bother caring either. Oh, nobody would outright flout Milady's wishes, but it was *so* easy to come up with an excuse to stop by for five minutes, and since everyone else was doing it...?

Milady ought to have known, I thought darkly, when at last Val grew tired of this and closed the library. It was late in the evening by that time, and we had to turn people away at the door. I did not ask where Val stashed Bill for the night; I only established that it was somewhere suitably fiendish by way of security, and properly unguessable.

'You're sure nobody will find him?'

'Perfectly,' said Val wearily.

'He's behind a few stout locks, of course?'

'Of course. Will you please go to bed, Ves.'

'I'm going.' And I did, but I was back in half a minute. 'How many stout locks?'

'Several. *Go!*'

I went, but I passed an unsettled night, my head full of paranoid imaginings. See, I have never been involved with such a spectacular find before. The pressure weighed upon me rather more than I cared to admit to anybody. Upon rising the following morning, I strove to erase the signs of a poor night's rest from my face, or at least to draw attention away from them through the use of my sparkliest cosmetics.

I was accordingly a little late reaching the dining area. It's a bit school-cafeteria down there, to be honest, with great cauldrons of food lined up behind a long series of counters, and little clusters of tables spread about the floor. But they have a way of serving all my favourites — a positive feast of berries this morning, and an entire vat of yoghurt, the full-fat kind — so I don't much mind.

Jay was already seated at our usual table near the biggest window. He had Indira with him. Val was also there, and Rob, and Nell. They looked formidably as though they were holding an emergency council, which hardly seemed reasonable at that hour of the morning.

When I reached the table with my bowl of breakfast delights, I saw a newspaper spread out in the centre. They were the colour pages from the front, the headlines, and my heart sank like a stone because there in enormous letters was the announcement: 'Spectacular Find at the Society!'

And Bill's picture.

5

'Morning!' I said brightly, and slumped into the vacant chair at Jay's elbow. 'Disaster?'

'Not quite,' said Jay, and awarded me half a piece of toast slathered in peanut butter. 'Just some, uh, sub-optimal developments.'

To be honest with you, I really don't need feeding up; I'm quite comfortably proportioned as it is. But who can resist peanut butter on toast? I skipped over the question of Jay's inscrutable motives in sharing his food with me — trying not to notice that he was doing the same for Indira — and focused on the article instead. It was light on information and heavy on rumour, but it had the salient facts down: a book featuring a previously unheard of, and extremely powerful, enchantment had come to light, and stood to revolutionise the way magickal libraries operated. They had spared no efforts to promote the story to its widest extent; every page glittered with come-hither-and-read magick.

To my further dismay, there was another picture inside: Jay holding the book.

I jabbed a finger at it. 'Who took that?'

'No idea,' said Rob grimly. 'But it must have been somebody at Home.'

I glowered into my berry-bowl, and comforted myself with a spoonful of yoghurt. It was one thing for the Society's members to be a bit too seduced by the marvels of Bill to resist making a trip to see him; it was quite another to sell the story to the media, complete with photos.

'Does Milady know?' I asked.

'We're preparing a delegation,' said Rob.

Hence the leaden atmosphere at the table. We were all going to get it in the neck.

'Straight to bed, and without any supper,' I said glumly.

'A thousand lines each,' added Val. '*I must not reveal the Society's secrets to the newspapers.*'

Jay said, 'How long before we get the swarms of reporters beating down the doors?'

'No need to worry about that,' said Rob. 'The House is pretty hard to find, if you're not familiar with the route.'

Jay looked sceptical. 'Journalists have a way of getting around problems like that.'

Val set down her mostly-empty coffee cup with a snap. 'One disaster at a time, if you please.'

'Sorry,' said Jay, contrite. 'Milady first, reporters later.'

THE FIRST PERSON DRAGOONED into the role of peace envoy was Nell, seeing as she is our media co-ordinator and suchlike. I don't actually know what her official job title is, if she even has one. She manages a lot of our technical requirements — she's spent decades building a huge data-base of basically everything we know that we know, and her team fixes all the tech bits that go wrong. She's also responsible for our internet presence (such as it is), which means our website and social media. That makes her our PR person, right? She'll be spending half of *her* morning putting together the kind of press release that puts out fires, or so we hope.

The second person volunteered for duty was yours truly.

'You're so good at it, Ves,' said Nell, fidgeting with her glasses. She had a second pair tucked into the coiffed coils of her grey hair; did she know? Apparently I was not the only person feeling wrong-footed by the events of the night.

'What, exactly, am I good at?' I said, trying not to sound quite so frosty as I felt.

'Making things sound good,' said Nell bluntly.

'Charming people,' muttered Jay.

'Persuading Milady to let you off,' said Rob, though since he teamed his comment with a smile of genuine affection I felt less like kicking him than I did the others.

'You talk a good talk, Ves,' Val said, arranging herself upon the side of my enemies without a trace of apology. 'It's one of your talents.'

'Lucky me,' I muttered.

I looked at Indira, in case she wanted to join in with the stone-throwing. But she stared back at me with big, guarded eyes and said nothing at all.

She looked, to my horror, as though she were more frightened of *me* than the rest of us were of Milady-in-anger.

I set that problem aside.

'Fine,' I said, magnificently gracious. 'Your poor, beleaguered Ves will sally forth and take a few bullets while the rest of you... what?'

'Review security,' said Rob.

'Figure out what in the world to do with Bill,' Val put in.

I looked at Jay, who shrugged. 'I'll come with you.'

'What? Voluntarily?'

'Why not?'

I narrowed my eyes. 'You've seen how hard everybody else worked to get out of this.'

'Except you.'

'I've been betrayed by my own troops, sent forth as sacrificial victim—'

'But with backup.'

I smiled, rather touched. 'That's kind. *So* kind I'd even give you that toast back, if I hadn't already eaten it.'

Jay wrinkled his nose. 'Er, no need to go to extraordinary lengths.'

In the event, Milady wasn't even angry. But she was extremely alarmed, which was far worse.

'Tell me everything,' she ordered, when Nell and Jay and I had trailed into her tower-top room and stood lined up on the carpet like a row of naughty children.

We did, though not in any coherent fashion. Milady listened to our fragmented account of the previous day's happenings in a taut silence that I found excessively uncomfortable. When we arrived at the developments of the morning, and held up the newspaper for her perusal, the air practically vibrated with tension.

When at last we stopped talking over each other, interpolating corrections upon each other's narratives and generally confusing everything, Milady went so long without speaking that I began to wonder whether we'd lost her altogether.

At last, she spoke, and though her words emerged in her usual crisp fashion, and with every appearance of total composure, I could hear a note of something else lying behind them; something like fear. 'While I appreciate Rob's confidence in the elusiveness of this house, and his no doubt excellent efforts to assure our security within it, I must disagree with his conclusions. You are quite right, Jay: those with a strong enough motive to find us will surely contrive a way. That goes for reporters, and some other, rather more unsavoury characters as well. It is my conviction that this troublesome book must be taken out of the House at once, and conveyed to a safer spot.'

That caused a little stir. I exchanged a foreboding look with Jay, who looked as worried as I felt.

'Jay, as our Waymaster, you are able to carry the book farther and faster than anybody else. I encourage you to choose a destination entirely at random; that way, it will be harder for others to guess the book's location, and all but impossible for anyone to follow in any timely fashion. Do not linger at any henges. Take Ves with you; she is a woman of significant resources and will be able to resolve any difficulties that arise.

'Nell, it falls to you to make a suitable announcement. By all means, confirm the find; it is too late to hope to deceive anyone on that score. Don't try to play down either its significance or potential. What I want you to do is to mention, as casually as you can, that the book is no longer at Home. I am not at all concerned what excuse you come up with to explain its removal, provided only that it is unexceptionable. The more mundane, the better. I would not have anybody coming *here* expecting to find that book, nor do I wish it to be known that we are expecting exactly such an attempt.'

This barrage of instructions left all three of us a little stunned. I, being Ves the Glib (apparently) recovered my wits first, and said: 'Forgive me, Milady, but why *are* we expecting such an attempt?' I mean, I'd had no trouble grasping Bill's importance to the magickal communities of Britain, but Milady was talking as though serious trouble was not only likely but inevitable.

Her response was swift, crisp and disdainful. 'Ves. Nell. You have been with us long enough to be only too aware that we are not the only organisation in this country with an interest in ancient magickal artefacts. And you are as well aware that they do not all operate upon the same motives.'

'Chancers, rogues and thieves, the lot of them,' I murmured for Jay's benefit.

'Quite,' said Milady. 'Not all of our rival organisations can fairly be described in such terms, of course, but one or two of them can. In particular, you may have heard rumours of a new group calling themselves Ancestria Magicka.'

Jay choked. 'Really?!'

'I've heard of them,' I confirmed, rolling my eyes. 'Treasure hunters, the worst kind. No respect for heritage. Pirates, if you will.'

'Snappy name,' muttered Jay.

'Formed last year, they have swiftly grown in both power and ambition. I have not made it generally known across the Society, but since January of this year there have been three known attempts by members of Ancestria Magicka to infiltrate our House. They were all foiled by the efforts of Rob Foster and his excellent team, and we do not yet know what, precisely, was their goal. Was it espionage? Theft? And more importantly, have there been other attempts that were successful enough to escape detection altogether?

'The news that somebody from among our own ranks has been responsible for giving news and photographs to the press is a matter of some concern to me. It might have been done thoughtlessly, or it might have been the product of something much more reprehensible. The House itself may be able to provide some information upon this point, and I shall investigate that possibility as soon as possible. But in the meantime, I cannot feel that the book is as safe here as I would like. Its presence here is an open invitation to Ancestria Magicka, and to any other group with similar ambitions. Are there any questions?'

Jay said, 'How long do I have to dance about the country with Bill?'

'You'll be notified when it is safe to return, or you may be called upon to hand off the book to somebody else. You will receive information, Jay.'

'Right.'

'Er,' I said. 'When you spoke of my "resolving difficulties", what exactly did you have in mind?'

'I hardly know, Ves, but Jay's picture with the book has been helpfully spread around, hasn't it? I do not know whether his status as Waymaster is broadly known outside of the Society, but it may well be. It is not impossible that somebody may guess, therefore, what we would do with the book, and come for you. That is why I advise staying away from the henges.'

'In that case I'd like Rob with us, really,' I said, though with only faint hope.

'I cannot spare Rob at this time. He is needed here. But consider yourself approved to take whatever you want from Stores. I know that will please you.'

It did, for I was rarely given so complete a carte blanche. *Whatever I want* meant anything at all, up to and including the shiniest, most powerful toys.

'I want a wand,' I said.

'Take the Sunstone.'

THE SUNSTONE WAND IS one of the Society's prizes. It is a beautiful object, made from spangled Norwegian sunstone all fitted up with silver filigree (well, it *was* made in the nineteenth century, and they were not known for their restrained sense of the aesthetic). It is shorter than you might expect. The long, thin, delicate wands of popular imagination are lovely to look at, but hard to carry around without getting them broken. The Sunstone Wand was made to be used, not just admired, so it is only about a foot in length, and sturdy at half an inch thick.

Wands are popular for channelling magickal energies in all manner of useful ways, but a real wand — the kind you spell with a capital W — is a rare and fine thing indeed. *Those* Wands are made from pure crystal, crafted by a master Spellwright, and they tend to be heirlooms.

I presented myself at Stores in a state of such anticipation I was forgetting to breathe.

This time, Ornelle was there.

'Back already?' said she, eyeing me with the kind of suspicion I have in *no* way deserved.

I eyed her right back. Ornelle's one of the few trolls regularly employed by the Society (most of the others are cooks). She's splendidly sized and invariably splendidly dressed, with a penchant for big, dangly jewellery. A fellow magpie, she's been in charge of Stores for years, and she is ferociously protective of the contents.

I usually try to slip by when she's not there.

'Milady sent me for supplies,' I said, and tried (futilely) to make my short self look just a little bit taller.

'All right.' Ornelle slipped on a pair of bejewelled glasses and took up a clipboard. She proceeded to escort me every step of the way, and made notes about everything I took up. Infuriating. I may sometimes be slow about bringing things back but I'm not a *thief*.

She made some difficulty about the Wand.

'You need the Sunstone again?' There was an offensive emphasis on the word *again*.

'Again!' I echoed in outrage. 'I've only had it once before and that was three years ago!'

'And it took you almost six weeks to bring it back.'

'I needed it for a while.'

'And this time?'

'I don't know. I'm being sent out into the wilds of Britain with a protégé and an artefact to protect, not to mention my own hide. It might take some time.'

Ornelle wanted to make trouble, I could see that she did. But for all that she sometimes distrusts me, she knows I wouldn't outright make up an order from Milady. Who would be mad enough to do that? The truth will always out.

She wrote down: "Sunstone Wand to Cordelia Ves" in big, blocky letters and underlined it, with the date written beside.

When I made to leave, she blocked my way. 'Vesper,' she said very seriously.

'Ornelle.'

'If anything untoward happens to that Wand, I'm re-possessing everything you've ever been given.'

Everything? 'You mean like my tea cup?' It's enchanted. Gives a different flavour of tea every time.

'Like your tea cup.'

'And the Curiosity that does my hair?'

'Everything.'

I gulped. 'I will defend it with my life.'

I didn't need such an admonition, of course — we would all defend artefacts like the Sunstone Wand with our lives. That's what we're for. But Ornelle required re-assurance, and apparently felt pacified.

'Best of luck,' she said as she cleared out of my way.

I wasn't sure whether she was talking to me or the Wand, but I answered anyway. 'Thanks.'

6

Jay was waiting for me down in the Waymastery Station. I don't suppose anybody else calls it that but me, but it's what it is. Unprepossessing, for all its exalted purpose: just a tiny room in the cellar, unpainted and virtually unfurnished. There's an ancient henge under the floor, and that's what Jay uses to whizz us about.

He had a small shoulder bag with him, which he opened when I came in. I took a peek inside, and saw a cloth-wrapped bundle snugly nestled within.

'Bill?' I ventured.

'Bill,' Jay confirmed.

I patted the bag I carried over my own shoulders. 'I've got your stuff.' Change of clothes, life-saving magickal artefacts, the usual. Indira had dutifully packed up his personal things and left them out for me, while Jay was off securing the book. I could well imagine his task was not an easy one; nobody wanted to see Bill go, and he had to try to squirrel him away without anybody noticing besides. Anyone but Val, that is.

'Ready?' I said, watching Jay's face. He looked worried. A heavy frown creased his brow, and he couldn't stand still.

'Absolutely,' he said, fidgeting with the strap of his bag.

'Except?'

The frown deepened. 'I'm worried about Indira.'

'She'll be fine. It's not like there's an army of orcs marching upon the House, or anything.'

'I'm worried about what happens to her if anything happens to me.'

Oh. 'Er, that's a bit doomy,' I tried. 'We're not in mortal danger.'

'Then why the Sunstone?'

'*Bill* is in mortal danger.' I said this in a whisper, hoping that the book was too well wrapped-up to hear me. '*We* aren't.'

'She's shy. It's hard for her to manage without me.'

'Even for a week or two? She needs to stand on her own feet sometime, Jay, or she'll never be independent.'

He scowled at that; I'd irritated him. 'Let's go, anyway.'

'If I may be permitted my opinion,' said Bill, his voice doubly muffled by the cloth wrappings and the bag. 'The little Spellwright is in no danger, either of harm or morti-fication.'

'How do you know?' said Jay snappishly.

'She and I have had conversation together. I found her to be bright-minded, and more resilient than elder brothers are inclined to imagine.'

The fact that Bill and Indira had been chatting together was news to me, though perhaps not to Jay, for he just gave me a sideways look and then went on with his preparations to leave. 'I hope you're right,' he said to Bill. I have no idea what he does when he's making ready to use the Ways, so I just stand back and try to keep out of his way.

A breeze picked up in the room, and began to build. 'Off we go,' said Jay, and held out a hand to me.

I took it. Since I met Jay, I have had a little practice at travelling the Ways. Enough to know that it is a disorient-ing experience, and can leave a person feeling unpleasantly shaken up in the middle. It appears to have an even greater impact upon Jay, but he went about his work with an en-viable composure, and betrayed no further signs of unease.

I do wish he had warned me before departure, however. Last time, we had waited until the Winds of the Ways had gathered themselves to quite a height before we set off. This time, the breeze had barely doubled in strength. There I was, tranquil enough yet in the expectation of its being a few more minutes before we would be going anywhere—

—and then I was away, tossing about in the wind like a miserable little leaf and clinging fiercely to Jay while the currents rattled my teeth and did awful things to my hair.

When the winds died down, they left us marooned on top of a low hill looking out over an expanse of drab fields. Stone monuments rose around us, which at first glance I took to be your typical ancient megalithic arrangement — except that, at a second look, the stones looked oddly new.

'I forgot to ask where you were taking us,' I said, a little breathless.

'Milton Keynes.' Jay sat cross-legged upon the ground in a pose of studied nonchalance, and looked around with more apparent satisfaction than I was feeling.

'Milton Keynes.' I got to my feet and took a couple of breaths, waiting until my knees steadied.

'Yes.'

'But *why.*'

'Because of all the places you and I might heroically flee with a magickal book, who'd ever think of Milton Keynes?'

Who indeed. 'And what in the name of Milady's garters is this?' I flicked a finger at the nearest lovely, smooth stone.

'A new henge.'

'*A new henge?*'

'It isn't their age that makes them effective, you know.' Jay picked himself up with some care, and squared his shoulders. 'Built last decade. Part of the city plan.'

One of the hazards of my trade: a tendency to start making overly simplified and accordingly fallible suppositions, for example: the older, the better. 'I suppose it's about as reasonable as putting in a train station.'

Jay's lips quirked in a smile. 'If only there were a few more Waymasters to make use of them. Somebody had dewy-eyed ideas about training up a lot more of us.'

'Can't manufacture that kind of talent.'

'Apparently not. You okay?'

'Of course!' If Jay was determined to be Totally Fine then so was I. I looked around at the uninspiring landscape, and hoisted my bag higher upon my shoulder. 'What now?'

'I don't know. Fancy a cup of tea?'

'Last one to the cafe's a rotten egg.' I began to totter down the hill.

'Which cafe?'

'Any!'

But my phone buzzed before I was more than halfway down the hill, and I hastily grabbed it.

'Ves?' said Val. 'Are you all right?'

'Perfectly. Why wouldn't I be?'

'And Jay?'

I looked round to check, if it would make Val happy, and saw Jay wandering down the hill some way behind me, hands in the pockets of his ever-present leather jacket. 'He's fine. Val, what's the matter?'

Val exhaled in a way that filled me with an unreasonable foreboding. How could I be so unsettled by a sigh? 'Milady had me pull up everything we know about Ancestria Magicka, which proved to be embarrassingly little. So then she had me go comb the world for every new scrap of information I could find — in fact she put the entire library staff on it, and—'

'Val, the suspense is killing me.'

'Sorry. Ves, they have a Waymaster.'

I almost dropped the phone. 'What? How's that possible?'

'Imported her from Hungary. She's been on the job only slightly longer than Jay, but she knows her stuff. Graduate from a top magickal university, comes highly recommended, entire bidding war to employ her. Etc. I'm sending pics. Her name's Katalin Pataki.'

'And you think they'll send her after us.'

'Well, wouldn't you? Why did they go to such lengths to get a Waymaster on the staff, if not for occasions like this?'

'They can't possibly know where we are, though, can they? Jay picked a destination at random, like Milady said.

What are they going to do, travel to every single henge in the entire British Isles looking for us?'

'Ves, I don't have time to convey everything I've lately learned about this lot, but I'd advise against underestimating them. They may be new, but they've already got Milady worried.'

Curses. 'Thanks, Val.'

'Be careful.'

I checked the pictures and then put my phone away, a variety of thoughts flitting across my mind. Who *were* these people? They had gone pretty far afield in search of a Waymaster, and poured buckets of money into securing one. Why?

And if they had those kinds of resources to throw around after less than a year... who the hell was funding them?

'Jay,' I said when he reached me. 'We may have a problem.'

'Another one?'

I relayed Val's news, but Jay did not react as I'd expected. He thought for a moment, frowning deeply, and then said: 'A bidding war?'

'That's what she said.'

'A *bidding war*?' He looked thunderstruck. 'You know, my parents told me not to take the first offer I received. They *told* me.'

'So why did you?'

'The Society's legend. How could I refuse?'

'Then it's no good regretting that your salary isn't higher. Can we talk about this later?'

'Right.' Jay shook himself and began to march off, heading for who-knew-where, but after a few paces he slowed again. 'Was Bill under guard all night?'

'No idea. Ask Bill.'

Jay began to root furiously through his bag, and at last extracted the book, stripped of its cloth wrapping. 'Bill, have you been left alone at any time in the past twelve hours or so?'

'No, sir!' said Bill brightly. 'I have been very much admired, and without pause, ever since the news of my existence was gratifyingly taken up.'

'By whom?' I said, warily.

'Oh, by everyone! My acquaintance has expanded enormously.'

'Did anyone tamper with you?' said Jay.

'Decidedly not!' said Bill, outraged at the very idea.

But Jay was not satisfied, and neither was I. 'The problem with Orlando,' he said, turning Bill around in his hands, 'is that he's sometimes too clever by half. Those pearl-things you've got, for example; even a non-magicker could use them. A potent spell perfectly encapsulated inside something inoffensive; no particular skill required to use it, and therefore no discernible trace left for a paranoid Waymaster to discern, or even a touchy, overly talkative grimoire of a book...' As he spoke he was inspecting Bill's covers and turning over page after page, ignoring the book's protests that he was a grimoire of enormous ability and no one could conceal a spell between his own pages and hope to escape detection.

'Ah,' said Jay then, and took up something that sparkled when he held it up to the afternoon sunlight. It was round, and about an inch across; pale and translucent, so much so that I wondered Jay had spotted it at all. The kind of thing, in short, that no one would much take note of. If you didn't know better, you might have said it was some kind of sticker, or a patch, or perhaps a bookmark.

'That's a tracker spell,' I gasped. I had seen them before. Orlando's technicians craft a lot of them, and they're wildly popular across the Society. These aren't the type of thing even a non-magicker could use, but they're among the simplest of charms to manipulate, requiring only a trickle of magick.

Jay tossed it to me. It lay in my palm, warm and faintly buzzing.

I dropped it at once.

'We'd better go.' Jay spoke tersely, already packing Bill away into his bag again.

'My most abject apologies!' Bill was babbling as Jay closed the bag upon him. 'I had no notion—'

'Not your fault, Bill,' I said. 'You've been out of the game for four centuries.' I was looking around as I spoke, as though I expected some kind of obvious course of action to occur to me if I moved my neck and blinked enough.

Blank mind. Palpitating heart. Not good.

'It doesn't matter where we go as long as we go *quickly*,' said Jay, and departed at a jog.

But he was too late, for a flicker of movement atop the hill caught my eye. I stopped, squinting against the light. What was it, a bird? Or worse?

'*Ves!*' yelled Jay behind me.

It was not a bird. A woman stood up there, her figure indistinct in the distance, but I could discern enough to be sure. She matched the photos Val had sent: tall, a shade too thin, long dark hair.

She had a man with her, too. He was holding what looked unpromisingly like a Wand.

I turned tail, and ran like a rabbit after Jay.

7

By the time I reached Jay, I was already scrambling to retrieve my syrinx pipes. Rooting around inside your own underwear is an inelegant business, but I had not the leisure to care just then. *Why* do the damned things have to wriggle around so much in there? It's not like there is much room to manoeuvre; I cannot be said to be incapable of properly filling out a brassiere.

Fortunately, Jay has observed this process before.

'Behind us!' I panted, and then wished I had not, for Jay took one look and sped up into a proper sprint, and soon began to draw away from me.

'*Stop!*' I yelled. 'We can't outrun them, idiot!' They were gaining on us already, not least because Katalin, curse her, had legs about three times as long as mine.

There — I had it. My fingers touched metal, and I drew out my tiny silver pipes, warm from their snug little hiding place. I set them to my lips and played an urgent melody, no easy task while I was still moving.

Jay didn't stop, but he did slow down. 'How long does it usually take Addie to—'

He didn't need to finish the sentence because Adeline, my beauty, was already whistling down from the skies, her silvery-white coat glittering in the sun. Addie, a rare winged unicorn, and my friend of some years.

'I asked her to hurry,' I said and ran forward to meet her. I was up on her back in seconds and ruthlessly hauled Jay up behind me. Catching hold of the silver rope she's kind enough to wear, I gasped, 'Away, Addie! Doesn't matter where, so long as it's fast.'

She leapt, her huge wings flapping, and we were airborne. Jay clung to me with one arm and clutched Bill with the other, while I kept my anxious gaze upon Katalin and her companion.

'Oh, no...' I muttered after a moment.

'What!' yelled Jay.

'That man! He's got a Wand and he's... yes, I really think he's going to—'

A missile like a tiny, crackling lightning bolt shot past my nose. 'He *is*!' I gasped, outraged.

'They're *shooting at us*?' Jay shouted.

I was too busy scrabbling for my Sunstone to reply.

'What was that you were saying about not being in mortal danger?!'

'I acknowledge myself mistaken upon that point.' I had the Wand out by that time, and as Addie gathered herself and put on an extra burst of speed, I mustered my wits, my resolve and my magick and sent an answering shot back. Then several more for good measure; I *was* feeling a trifle irritated.

I had the satisfaction of seeing Katalin's companion drop his Wand and go on the retreat, arms raised.

My next missile hit him in the stomach, and he dropped.

'Hah!' I crowed, arms raised. 'It's victory for the Sunstone Team!'

'Don't celebrate too early,' cautioned Jay, which was not unreasonable of him, but quite unnecessary. Addie was flying like a bolt of lightning herself by that time, and the two Ancestria Magicka agents soon diminished into tiny, indeterminate specks and disappeared from sight.

I glanced down at the city of Milton Keynes spread out below us. 'Miserable spot, but there's probably some good tea down there somewhere.'

Jay shook his head. 'Too close. We'd better fly on a while.'

Addie bore us generally west. We passed over a number of villages, and when the larger sprawl of Buckingham (thank you, phone) came into view we decided to land.

That part is always tricky; where to come down that's sufficiently discreet? It's always inconvenient when local papers start reporting unicorn sightings. But Addie's far cleverer than I and found us a tree-shaded spot a short walk from the outskirts of the town.

I checked her carefully to make sure she hadn't been hit. She was unharmed, but she was also displeased with me.

'Sorry,' I told her, shame-faced. 'I did not expect to come up against a lightning-throwing Wand-wielding sidekick.'

We left her drinking her fill from a charming river, her silvery sides heaving with exertion. There was plenty of grass about for her to snack upon, and better yet, some tasty-looking spring flowers.

I kissed her nose before we wandered off. 'Best unicorn ever.'

Addie flicked her ears at me, and decisively bit through a sunny narcissus flower. The first of many, I had no doubt.

'Eat them all!' I encouraged as we walked off. 'You've earned them!'

'You're a terrible unicorn parent,' was Jay's verdict upon my behaviour. 'She'll be sick if she eats all those flowers.'

'How do you know?'

Jay had no answer to that.

We found a tea-room in Buckingham and partook liberally of its finest beverages (and a cake or two. How could I help it, when they were serving carrot cake *and* Victoria sponge?). The first thing Jay did (after gulping down a liberal quantity of reviving tea) was to take out Bill and comb through his pages more minutely than before. 'Try not to get too chatty, Bill,' he said in an undertone. 'The people here would be more horrified than charmed by a talking book.'

'Non-magickers?' Bill whispered.

'I'm afraid so.'

There were not many people besides us, thankfully: a pair of elderly ladies having afternoon tea at a window table, and a middle-aged man in a suit drinking coffee and reading a newspaper. None of them paid us the smallest attention.

I could still wish Bill's whisper somewhat less penetrating. 'Am I correct in supposing that I was almost absconded with a little while ago?' he demanded.

'Quite incorrect,' I said with dignity. 'We rescued you in the nick of time.'

'I am glad to hear it. I should not like to fall again into the hands of villainy.'

It took me a moment to remember what he meant by *again*: John Wester, of course, with his grave-robbing tendencies.

While Jay was thus employed, I called Val, and informed her in hushed tones of everything that had happened.

'Crap,' she said, succinctly.

'It was, rather. But we're fine.'

'I'll tell Milady. In light of what you've just said, I doubt she will object to sending Rob after you.'

'I wouldn't mind some help,' I admitted.

'Keep me informed of your whereabouts.'

'Will do.' I hung up.

'I don't see any more tracking charms,' Jay said, and handed Bill off to me. 'Want to check as well?'

I did so, enjoying the feel of Bill's exquisite vellum pages under my hands. They don't make books like that anymore. I reached the end without finding anything untoward, either; but that brought me face-to-face with John Wester's clumsily-sketched map and its label: Drogryre.

I handed Bill back to Jay, thinking. 'Why did John Wester want to find that grave?' I mused aloud. 'Specifically? Bill says he's an opportunist, but he must have had some reason to fix upon that particular spot.'

Jay opened his mouth, but blinked and hesitated. 'Er,' he said.

'Right? Why did he think there was something valuable in there with her?'

'Sometimes people were buried with valuable objects?' suggested Jay.

'That might be it, if she was wealthy. Was she, Bill?'

'Not particularly. My erstwhile mistress did achieve some modicum of prosperity by the end of her life, due to her being in increasingly high demand. But she began destitute, and never arrived at anything that might be termed wealth.'

I frowned. 'So why did Wester think her grave was so important?'

'Are you sure it's her grave that's marked here, Bill?' said Jay, tapping the heavily-inked X with one finger.

'Quite certain. He spoke of it endlessly.'

Reminded of the early journal entries, Jay flipped back to the front of the book. But he was soon obliged to abandon his efforts to make it out, and gave it instead to me.

I saw his problem at once. Neither of us had yet had chance to take a close look at those entries; once we had realised how precious Bill was himself, the scribblings of a thief like Wester had ceased to seem important. I now saw that Wester's musings were written in a style of English which predated anything we might consider easily comprehensible; virtually Chaucerian, in fact. And his handwriting was abominable.

'Of course it's Middle English,' I said with a sigh. 'Zareen said as much. I can read it, but not easily, and not here.'

'We shouldn't linger here any longer, either,' said Jay. 'The trackers may be gone but Katalin and Co. saw the direction we were heading in, and we aren't that far from Milton Keynes.'

I agreed to this without much regret, having finished my tea and sustenance some time since. We packed up and left. I considered retrieving Addie and flying onward, but there were a few objections to that idea, not the least of which was that she was already unhappy with me. So we got on a bus, and spent the rest of the day dawdling dully from town to town by way of a series of rattling, pootling old vehicles. It was quite peaceful, considering the events of earlier in the day, and since nobody showed up to try to wrest Bill from us, neither Jay nor I had any real complaints.

We ended up at a bed-and-breakfast in a town called-Quainton, dined in true British fashion upon fish and chips, and then fell asleep in front of my TV.

I woke up just before dawn, and was pleased to note that Jay did not appear to be prone to snoring.

I woke again an hour or two later to find he had un-sprawled himself from the other side of my bed and gone back to his own, leaving me in full possession of all the space. This pleased me.

The fact that he had taken Bill with him did not please me nearly so much, as it ruined my plans of having a private chat with the book. I wanted to examine him some more on the topic of Drogryre, her life, and especially her death, in case he should be able to shed any more light on the activities of John Wester. That would have to wait.

I wandered down for breakfast, half expecting to find Jay already there; he was usually an early riser, like me. But I was served with cereal, yoghurt, toast and eggs alone, despite the fact that it was well past eight o' clock.

I took my tea upstairs and tapped upon Jay's door.

No answer.

'Jay?' I put my ear to the door, but heard nothing.

I tried the handle, and finding the door unlocked (... not good), I went in.

No Jay. He was not in the bathroom, either.

What *was* still there was all of his belongings — except for Bill. The shoulder-bag stood empty of book; even the cloth wraps were gone. His favourite leather jacket, the dark one so well-loved its cuffs and collar were scuffed, hung over one of the brass bed-posts.

I stood a moment in growing horror, trying to convince myself that there was some plausible, non-terrifying explanation for the dual and unscheduled absence of both Jay and Bill.

There was not, of course.

8

I RAN DOWNSTAIRS.

The landlady only confirmed my worst fears: she had seen nothing of Jay all morning, not a peep since yesterday evening. She had not heard anything in the night that might have sounded suspiciously like a break-in by magickal marauders; but then, neither had I. At dawn, Jay had been sleeping comfortably in front of a desultorily flickering television. A couple of hours later, he'd vanished.

I stood in Jay's abandoned room, dithering like a ninny while my mind turned in confused circles. These are the moments in life when one would wish to be a picture of unflappable resolve, brimming with self-confidence and perfectly clear upon the best course of action. My brain would only consent to ask foolish questions. *Where was Jay?* No way to tell. *Why had he gone?* Well, he probably hadn't stepped out for coffee without his jacket, wallet or keys.

Then Rob showed up.

I was informed of his presence when my landlady — a mild retiree with a taste for forties fashions — stood diffidently on the tiny landing outside our rooms and called: 'Dear? There is a gentleman to see you.'

I thought first of Katalin's mysterious sidekick, and marched downstairs with my Wand in my hand, ready to wrest Jay from him by hook or by crook. But of course, the man patiently awaiting me in the hall was Rob. He was looking extra forbidding: with his dark frame swathed in even darker clothes, no wonder my landlady had seemed a bit nervous. He looked like the riot police, or maybe an assassin.

'No!' I yelped when I saw him, and stopped, frozen, two-thirds of the way down the stairs. 'Go away!'

'Morning, Ves,' said Rob, unperturbed. 'Why?'

'Because when I tell you what's happened you'll have to kill me.'

'I might kill *somebody*,' Rob allowed — not at all to the reassurance of my poor landlady, who was, at that moment, creeping past us into the safety of her living-room. 'But never you. What's the matter?'

'I've lost the book.' I sat down heavily upon the stairs and clutched at my hair, whose jaunty pink colour seemed quite inappropriate just then.

Rob didn't move. 'That is unfortunate.'

'*And* I've lost Jay.'

That gave him greater pause. He blinked, uttered, 'Ah,' and fell silent.

'Just make it quick,' I pleaded. 'I probably deserve to suffer, but I haven't the courage.'

Rob came forward and extended a hand. Reluctantly, I allowed myself to be hauled back to my feet. 'Calm, Ves,' he said, more kindly than I felt I deserved. 'It isn't your fault.'

'Of course it is! If I wasn't responsible for keeping them safe then who was?'

'Jay is not helpless.'

'He's never been sent out by himself yet. I'm here because I'm supposed to be competent. Milady said I could be relied upon to handle any "difficulties" that "might happen to arise"! And I haven't! I was *asleep*, and Jay was hauled off like a sack of potatoes!'

'Not necessarily.'

'What do you mean, not necessarily? That is *clearly* the case.'

Rob made no reply, exactly. He only said, 'Jay is clever,' which did not appear to relate to anything. 'Tell me what's happened.'

I brought him up to speed with as much detail as I could manage, finishing with, 'I don't even know how they found us in this wretched—' I broke off as a horrible idea occurred to me. I did not pause to explain; I merely turned and high-tailed it back up the stairs.

Jay's jacket. I all but tore it off the bedpost and rummaged through the pockets. Lots of detritus came out; I have too much respect for Jay's dignity to describe every article of it.

And there. At the bottom of his left pocket, hidden under a crumpled-up handkerchief, was a tiny round sparkling thing: one of Orlando's tracker charms.

'*Crap.*'

Rob had come in behind me. I handed it off to him without another word, and began to pace. How had it failed to occur to me to check Jay's clothes? Or my own! If someone had got close enough to Bill to stick a tracking-charm on him, it wasn't so far-fetched to imagine that the same someone might have done something similar to Jay. According to the news, at least, he was both the discoverer and the keeper of the precious book.

I engaged in a hasty scout of my own attire, courtesy of my lovely spangled Sunstone. It was a rather menial duty for such a magnificent heirloom, but the Wand was remarkably effective at detecting magick. I came up with nothing, or nothing besides the usual: the charmed ring I wear that adjusts the colour of my hair, the spell that keeps ladders from forming in my tights, that kind of thing. No trackers.

'I suppose they only wanted Jay,' I said, stashing the Wand.

'I wonder why.' Rob had gone quiet and tense in that focused way he has, and was examining the contents of Jay's abandoned room like a police detective. He called somebody. 'We have a mole at Home,' he said into it, tersely. 'Someone got a tracker-charm onto Jay, as well as the book, and they're both missing. Vesper's unharmed. Tell Milady.'

I began to feel calmer. Rob has that effect: he's completely unflappable.

So am I, usually, or at least more so. But I'd never lost a priceless artefact and a protégé in one day before.

'Where is the nearest henge?' said Rob next.

I caught his train of thought at once. 'Yes! They'd want to whisk off right away, wouldn't they? The easiest thing would probably be to go back to Milton Keynes.' I could not say this with any great certainty; I am after all legendary for my inability to find my way around.

Rob delicately refrained from saying this, though he did take the precaution of checking my theory on his phone. 'Milton Keynes it is,' he said, and fell to gathering up Jay's things. 'Let's go.'

I whistled up Addie again, and one of her friends, too — a sturdy stallion Rob's ridden before. We made the trip back to Milton Keynes' shiny new henge in record time, but we were still too late. The hilltop was a grey, empty space, an overcast morning and my disappointed hopes combining to render it a desolate scene.

We waited a full hour, just in case we had somehow managed to beat Jay's abductors to the site. But nobody came.

Rob was on his phone for a fair bit of this time, conveying the news to, and receiving advice from, various members of the Society. At length — bored, probably, of watching me hop anxiously about the hilltop like a rabbit on speed — he collected me up and escorted me kindly down the hill again. 'We're going Home,' he said, a shade grimly.

'How?'

'The boring way. By train.'

'What does Milady say?'

'Nothing about the immediate evisceration of one Cordelia Vesper, if that's what you mean.'

I heaved a small, inward sigh of relief. 'And what else?'

'Theories abound as to why Jay's vanished with the book, and—'

'Don't say it like that,' I begged, feeling compelled to interrupt. 'You make it sound like Jay thieved the book and ran.'

'Well, one or two people who dislike Jay are saying more or less that. But nobody who knows him would imagine it possible.'

'Who could dislike Jay?!'

'His unique skills put him in a powerful position, and power will always attract enemies.'

'Haters,' I muttered. I wondered suddenly whether Indira had heard the news. I hoped not, yet; much as I was at fault, I would rather tell her about her brother's disappearance myself. That way, I could make sure she was all right. Wherever he was, Jay would be worrying something awful about her.

'Milady's had Val researching Ancestria Magicka for the past two days,' Rob continued. 'She's now got the entire Research and Library Division on it, and has thrown them a lot of extra resources, to boot. She's confident they will soon come up with something that will help us to help Jay.'

'And Bill.'

'And Bill, though Jay is the Society's priority.'

I hoped this was because he's brilliant rather than because he's the first Waymaster we've had in nearly a decade.

'Also,' Rob added. 'Val said: Tell Ves to stop fussing.'

'Fussing?'

'Running around like a headless chicken.'

'I hope you told her that I am the very picture of cool composure, as always.'

Rob gave me a sideways look. 'Why would I ever tell her anything else?'

I patted his arm. 'I love you.'

'I know.'

WHEN WE ARRIVED HOME a few hours later, we went straight up to Milady's tower — the quick way. And by that I mean that House itself appeared to have got caught up in the sense of urgency Jay's vanishment had caused and gave us a lift straight up to the top. We went from the entrance hall to Milady's tower-top room in one step.

'Thank you, House,' I murmured. House and I have had a little conversation together before. I would not presume to call us friends, but we've been introduced, and one would never expect to sweep by an acquaintance unacknowledged.

'It's good to see you are well, Ves,' Milady greeted me.

I curtsied. 'I was in no danger, for they did not appear to want me.'

'An interesting point to note, indeed. Thank you for fetching her back so promptly, Rob. What have you both to report?'

'Nothing new,' Rob answered. 'We were not able to catch up with Katalin Pataki or her colleague, nor did we discover any clues as to Jay's whereabouts.'

'Is there any evidence that Pataki is behind the theft and kidnapping?'

'No solid evidence, though considering the encounter Jay and Ves had with those two yesterday, it seems too obvious a conclusion to be discounted.'

'I cannot disagree. Ves, I'd like you to go directly to Valerie, if you please. She may already have useful information to convey, and if not, your research skills will no doubt be wanted.'

'Yes, ma'am.'

'An attempt to recover Jay, and also the book, must be made very soon. I have sent envoys to Ancestria Magicka already in hopes of securing Jay's swift release by diplomatic means, if not the return of the book. But I cannot hold out much hope of its success; they are likely to meet only with a total denial of any involvement whatsoever. Therefore, our methods must be more direct.'

'Please tell me I am to be part of the team,' I said.

'I would not dream of excluding you, Ves. You will be very much needed.'

Phew.

'You also, Rob.'

Double phew. 'Is the identity of our traitor yet known?'

Milady's voice turned cold. 'Not yet.'

'It could be someone from Research.'

'And Valerie therefore has orders to collate all gleaned information discreetly, and to keep her silence on the topic of any planned response. As must the two of you.'

We readily agreed, of course, though I did so with a heavy heart. To have to keep secrets within my own organisation, and from people I have known for years! A painful duty.

I was reassured, though, to find that no suspicion had attached to *me*. If there were those who could doubt Jay's loyalty so far as to accuse him of stealing the book, well, I had my detractors, too. I had not lacked for opportunities to sabotage our little mission, and Jay's disappearance had happened while I was asleep in the very next room. Who was to say I hadn't had a hand in it all? I was comforted to find that Milady was in no way disposed to consider it likely, nor were Rob or Val.

It's good to have friends.

Vᴀʟ ɢʀᴇᴇᴛᴇᴅ ᴍᴇ ᴡɪᴛʜ a shrewd, narrow-eyed look. She sat behind her huge desk like a queen, as always; straight-backed, imperious, and far too knowing.

'Have you been eating?' she said.

I opened my mouth to protest that nothing — *nothing* — could long divide me and food, but then I realised I had not eaten since breakfast, and the prospect of doing so only induced a feeling of nausea.

So I swept this aside.

'I've been sent to help,' I said brightly. I tried, as I crossed to Val's desk, to walk with the supreme confidence of an unflappable woman, and took some comfort in the smart *rap-rap-rapping* sound my heels made upon the polished wooden floor.

Val was not convinced.

'Sit down before you fall over,' she said, with — was it, really? — a roll of her eyes.

My knees *were* feeling a bit weak, so I meekly obeyed. 'I feel so feeble.'

'Why, because you're worried? Come off it, Ves. You'd be equal to anything, if only it were *you* who'd been swiped. You'd be out of there in no time, pink hair flying, leaving the place a smoking ruin behind you. It's unusual for you to have to fear for someone else.'

It was the feeling of impotence that bothered me; I rarely felt so much at a loss. 'You don't... think they would harm him?' I hazarded.

'Never,' said Val with reassuring confidence. 'He is far too valuable.'

True. Waymasters do not grow on trees. 'What have you found out?'

'Right. Come with me.' Val glided out from behind her desk and sent her chair zipping for the main doors, an act which surprised me for a second. Chatting comfortably with Val at her own, name-plaqued desk was as customary as eating lunch.

But Milady's exhortation had not fallen upon deaf ears. I followed obediently behind Val's hovering chair — I tend to call it a wheelchair but only because it's the common parlance; the chair has no wheels because it flies. Val took me to my own hidden study carrel, and, with an air of mild disgust at the necessity, sealed it up with a slick silencing charm. The air sparkled in a way I found oddly reassuring; no one was going to be listening in on us.

Val tapped her impeccably-manicured fingernails upon the carrel's desk for a moment, apparently deciding where to begin.

9

'THEY'RE ELUSIVE,' VAL FINALLY said. 'Secretive to a fault, and yes, I am well aware of the irony of my calling *them* secretive when we are all employed by a woman whose sole identifiable presence consists of a disembodied voice and an old-fashioned mode of address. Nonetheless. Two days of digging and we don't have much.

'We know that Ancestria Magicka was formed last June, but we only know that because there was a brief press release about it in the Magickal Herald at the end of June. It described the organisation as "formed for the efficient, professional retrieval of artefacts of great cultural value" or something to that effect, and it puts a nice shine on what they do, but it didn't take long for them to develop a reputation for the kind of efficiency that consists more of smash-and-grab thuggery than sleek professionalism.

'We don't know who founded it or how they are funded, except that the Hidden Ministry certainly has no involvement. They are fully independent, which means largely unmonitored. We've found the names of only a few of their operatives, including Katalin Pataki. Her regular partner is George Mercer, who is known to carry a Sardonyx Wand. He was almost certainly the man you and Jay encountered at Milton Keynes.

'They've been recruiting aggressively. Milady revealed we have lost two prospective employees this year to superior offers from Ancestria Magicka. Considering the bidding war over Ms. Pataki, it's clear that they are not at all strapped for cash.'

Unlike us, I thought. We do all right, but that's about it, and we are more heavily reliant upon Ministry funding than Milady would like. *They are* so *interfering,* she had once complained to me, in an unusually forthcoming mood. With no such ties and no shortage of resources, Ancestria Magicka was in an enviable position indeed.

'Their goals remain unclear,' Val continued. 'They are rumoured to have secured at least two Great Treasures this year already, one at auction and one an original find, together with quite the list of lesser artefacts. But what they have done with them is anybody's guess. Sold them? Stashed them? Anything claimed by Ancestria tends to disappear without trace.'

I gripped the desk. '*Not* Jay.'

'This is the first I have heard of their absconding with a person. Crude as their methods are reported to be, they are not known for brutality. I imagine it likely that they have a clear purpose in mind for Jay.'

'Like ransom?'

'Unlikely. They do not need money, and while the Society is known to be in possession of some few Treasures ourselves, there are plenty still out in the world for them to pursue first, with greater ease and lesser risk. And why take only Jay, if all they wanted was a hostage? Why not you? You are a senior acquisitions specialist with quite the reputation outside the Society. They might well imagine your abduction would inspire a comfortable spirit of co-operation in Milady.'

I wondered if it would. Trying to mentally calculate one's own probable value to one's employers is a grisly business, however, so I soon abandoned the project.

I felt a little reassured by Val's logic, but it did not escape me that her recital had not yet included anything that might help us to find Jay. 'Where do they hide out?' I asked.

'Exactly.'

'Exactly?'

'I've spent all day on that very question, and I've had four other people on it, too. So's Nell. Ancestria Magicka has a pretty major internet presence, as it turns out; far more than we do. A slick, lovely website promoting their services in the best possible light, and carefully couched in terms that would not too much alarm any non-magicker who happened upon it. Nell's got a couple of people working on it, but without much progress. The website's registered to a shoe shop in Wolverhampton.'

'A shoe shop?'

'Currently specialises in orthopaedic shoes. Family business, established 1969.'

I put my head in my hands. 'Have you got anything useful at all?'

'Just one thing. Maybe.'

'A maybe thing.'

Val nodded. 'A year ago last February, a strange case came up in the property market: Ashdown Castle in Cheshire was suddenly sold. A fifteenth-century mansion with strong magickal connections ought not to have gone ownerless for very long, but the place was in a state of such near-total ruin that it was essentially valueless. I was surprised to hear of its sale, and even more surprised to learn that — by rumour at least — the sale price ran into the millions. The old place has some attractive heritage, to be sure; it's supposed to have been built by the Beaumonts, one of the most prominent magickal families of medieval England, and as with all such places it's said to be littered with history, old magick and secrets. But to pay several million for a ruin?'

'You think Ancestria Magicka bought it?'

'The idea occurred to me. They'd need a base of operations, and what better site for a group even more obsessed with all things old, obscure and priceless than we are? I thought little of the matter at the time, but I put it in my Mysteries folder and I dug it up this morning.' Val paused, perhaps for effect. 'There's little to be found about its new owners, which immediately made me more suspicious. All I could find was a name, or half a name — Becket. And guess who shares that surname?'

'Wha... oh. The shoe-sellers of Wolverhampton?'

'The same! Before you ask: no, I do not think that family has anything to do with it. They're squarely non-magickal, and characterised by the kind of dull respectability that absolutely precludes the possibility of such interesting shenanigans. I *do* think that our friends at Ancestria are going to extraordinary lengths to maintain secrecy about their doings, though, and they're probably using a few such unremarkable names and addresses as a blind.'

'It's thin,' I said.

'I know. But it's worth investigating.'

I nodded, distracted. Somebody had walked past our hideaway four times in the space of five minutes, back and forth, back and forth. A slim, shortish figure I recognised, moving at speed, her dark hair swinging.

'What's Indira doing?' I said, frowning.

'Looking for something,' murmured Val, and dissolved the protective charm around the carrel with a flick of her fingers.

I set off after Indira. I found her soon enough, for she was coming back my way yet again. She stopped when she saw me and gave me a wide-eyed stare.

'Hello,' I said cordially.

'I was looking for you,' said Indira.

'Here I am. What can I do for you?' I was trying to be as approachable as possible, and hoping I was not coming off as patronising. It was obviously too late to break the news of her brother's disappearance; her manner proclaimed she was already well informed.

Indira has the air of a schoolgirl as well as the appearance of one. She has been impeccably dressed every time I have seen her, but with none of Jay's flair. She wears neat, plain blouses and skirts, her hair always tied up into a perfect, severe ponytail. Her manner is self-contained and withdrawn; I might have called her reserved, if I didn't know she was shy. She looks as though she never knowingly puts a foot wrong, and wouldn't dream of doing so either, which makes the arm-sling an incongruous addition to her wardrobe.

I wondered what kind of person was hiding behind all that conscientious, slightly desperate perfection.

Indira put a phone into my hands. 'Jay's tracking charm is missing.'

I knew it for Jay's phone at once. Not because there was anything distinctive about it, as such; the latest iPhone, plain black case, the same thing at least fifty Society employees probably carried (Indira included). I knew it for Jay's because I had, only the week before, rather wickedly adorned it with a sparkly green butterfly sticker on the top left corner. For some reason, he'd left it there.

There was certainly no sign of a tracking charm anywhere on it. 'Does he always use them?'

Indira managed a tiny smile. 'He's always losing things. He was like that from a child. When he arrived here he got a whole batch of tracker-patches from Development and stuck them on everything he owns. I know, because he gave the leftovers to me.'

'He couldn't have just forgotten to put one on his phone?'

'No chance. The two items Jay loses the most often are his phone and his keys. They're the first things he would put trackers on.'

My hopes leapt for a second, until I remembered that Jay's keys had been in his jacket pocket, which was even now lying forlornly upon the bed in his empty room. 'Perhaps it fell off?' I suggested.

'They don't fall off.'

Indira spoke with certainty, and I had no power of arguing with her. Not being prone to misplacing my stuff, I have rarely had occasion to use them. 'You have some theory, I think?'

Indira hesitated. 'I think... he must have removed it deliberately. And if he did that, he has probably taken it with him.'

My mind raced, and came up blank. 'I don't know how they work. What do you do to locate the charm, if you have lost the object it's guarding?'

'They come in pairs. You keep one somewhere safe, and put its pair on whatever you want to keep track of. Then you can use one to lead you to the other. Jay's got an entire book of them.'

I began to feel the kind of wild, surging hope that tends to end in crashing disappointment, and did my best to contain it. 'Do you know where the book is?'

'No. That's why I came to you.'

'Forgive me, but you must know your brother far better than I.'

Indira's awkwardness manifestly tripled. She looked at her feet. 'I, um... cannot get into his room.'

Uh.

A vision of myself only an hour past drifted through my head. I had casually infiltrated Jay's room — skulked my way inside, in fact, since it *did* feel weird to be in there uninvited, and when Jay was absent. Feeling guiltily like an interloper, I'd placed his jacket and his other bits and pieces onto his bed and immediately fled. It had never occurred to me that he might have sealed off his room to everybody *but* me.

I could imagine well enough why he would keep that space private from a sister who had to be a least a decade his junior, however close they appeared to be. Why he would grant free access to me was a different problem, one I had no answer to whatsoever.

'He speaks highly of you,' said Indira to the floor.

Oh. 'Goodness, we aren't — it isn't like—'

'Oh, I know!' Indira hastily interjected, and with a degree of horror I could only find slightly insulting. 'I would never think *that*! I only meant that he trusts you.'

I let all of this pass; we were wasting time. 'Come on,' I said, and led the way smartly back to the main stairs. I had paid little close attention to all the flotsam and jetsam in Jay's pockets when I had made my frantic search before; I had been looking for a stray tracker-patch like the one Jay had found in the book, and nothing else had appeared relevant at the time. But I vaguely recalled the presence of a little booklet of some kind; I had probably mentally passed it off as a pocket notebook, however unnecessary such an accessory might be to a man with a smartphone. But that booklet, I was now willing to hope, contained all of Jay's paired tracking charms.

10

THE NEXT COUPLE OF hours got pretty exciting.

Indira and I hurried through the House to Jay's room. All the dorms are on the upper floors, and while there's space set aside for families (Miranda and Orlando, for example, have a suite of rooms they share with their daughter), the singles amongst us are housed in separate wings: one for the ladies, one for the gents.

What can I say. No one will be surprised to hear that Milady can be old-fashioned.

I'd had a bit of trouble finding Jay's room earlier in the day, and I wish I could say that the prior experience rendered it simple for me to find it again. It did not. I dithered and doubted and we wandered back and forth, but eventually found our way through the rabbit-warren of dormitories to the white-painted door which bore Jay's name. I unlocked it with a touch and in we went.

Or, in *I* went. Indira hovered in the doorway, trying not to look at anything. She need not have scrupled. Jay has only been with us for a few weeks, so he has not yet had time to personalise his room very much. It looks more or less as it was issued: a plain, white-painted chamber with a comfyish bed, chest of drawers, wardrobe, window over-looking the grounds. There were no pictures anywhere, few possessions strewn about; little, in short, to incriminate the owner in any fashion that might trouble either his sister or himself.

'He isn't going to mind,' I said to Indira, feeling mildly exasperated.

'If he wanted me in here he would have given me access.'

It was hard to argue with that, so I didn't try. I went straight to the jacket laid upon the bed and began a hasty riffle through its pockets; for all my stout words I would not feel entirely comfortable until I was safely on the right side of Jay's door again.

I found the booklet, withdrew it with hands that only slightly trembled, and flipped it open.

There inside were neat rows of translucent jellyish circles, glinting with magic.

'We've got them,' I told Indira, who sagged with relief. I put the booklet directly into her hands as I withdrew, and locked the door again behind me.

'Now what?' I said.

'I'll take this to Development. They aren't tuned to me, so they'll have to be cracked, and I'm only just learning—'

'Get it to Orlando.'

Indira blanched. '*Orlando*? But he's—'

'Dauntingly important, and eccentric to boot. I know. But he invented these things; nobody knows better than he how they work, and no one will get the job done faster. We have no time to waste.'

Indira looked ready to die of fright, but to her credit she mastered herself, and gave me what was probably meant to be an assured nod. 'Right.'

'I'd go with you,' I said, relenting a bit. 'But in this you have the advantage of me. I'm not allowed anywhere near Orlando's lab.'

She gave a lopsided, scared-looking smile, as though the prospect of her own relative importance to mine alarmed more than appeased her. 'Right,' she said again.

Away she went.

I was a little puzzled by her serene manner of talking about *cracking* Jay's tracking charms, but I was rapidly learning that Indira had a rather complicated sense of honour. Wresting the secrets from her brother's utility spells in order to rescue him from dire peril was one thing; *going into his room without permission* in order to secure the charms in the first place was quite another.

I spared a brief thought to wonder what manner of relationship those two had enjoyed through childhood, and went off to rejoin Val.

ABOUT HALF AN HOUR later, Indira was back. At a run.

The library was crowded, though surprisingly quiet for all that; everyone was variously intent upon their stacks of books, aged scrolls, or tab computers. Once in a while somebody went running for Val with some promising note, footnote, or anecdote, most of which were regretfully dismissed. Indira balked a moment at this vision of industrious humanity, but steeled herself far enough to make her way to the desk I had appropriated.

'Ves!' she said — very quietly, as though to be overheard by any of the people around me would be an unthinkable torment. 'Sutton Weaver.'

'What?' I put aside the book I'd been flipping through — a sixteenth-century traveller's journal wherein a woman called Alice Glover, engaged in jaunting through much of northern England, gave accounts of many of the great houses of the area, including some of those in Cheshire. I hadn't yet found any references to Ashdown Castle.

'Sutton Weaver,' repeated Indira. 'One of Jay's tracking charms is there, or about two miles distant. It's in—'

'I warn you,' I said, sitting up. 'If you say "Cheshire" I may kiss you.'

'Cheshire,' whispered Indira, backing quickly away.

I held up my hands. 'I didn't mean it.'

'Oh...' She collected herself. 'Um, Orlando's sent someone to Milady with the news.'

'Right. Let's go see Val.'

Val had Jay's location pinpointed within minutes. 'That,' she said with a scholar's relish, 'is Ashdown Castle.'

I felt elated, and also indignant. Milady's "diplomatic" measures had, as expected, achieved nothing; Ancestria Magicka emphatically denied having had anything to do with the disappearance of either Jay or Bill. They had even been so insulting as to commiserate with us on the loss of two such recent acquisitions (and to refer to Jay as an acquisition made me mad as fire). And they'd stashed him after all!

Val caught the look on my face. 'Remember, none of this is evidence.'

'I know. Just a series of incredible coincidences.'

'Yes.'

'You don't believe there's another explanation any more than I do.'

'Nope.'

I looked at Indira. 'Good job. Thank you.'

She blushed a shade or two darker. 'Um.'

I didn't wait for her to squirrel up some words. I was off to Milady, with the feeling that if she did not authorise an immediate expedition to pick up Jay, well, I was going anyway.

Val made me stop. 'Ves, Ashdown Castle won't be easy to find. It hasn't been marked on any map since the 1530s. It will be behind layers of spells for concealment, confusion, misdirection, everything.'

'I realise.'

'Much like this House.'

'What's your point?'

'How long did it take you to find us, when you first arrived?'

Two days, even with instructions. I did not want to have to say that out loud, not in front of Indira.

Val gave me a meaningful look. 'You'll need help. Don't bomb out of here in such a hurry that you forget that.'

I saluted, with only the mildest irony. She was, after all, quite right. 'Thanks, Val.'

Half an hour later, we were on the road. *We* consisted of me and Rob, travelling in my car (I own a Mini, the

Countryman sort. Blue. Yes, it's very beautiful). Ahead of us was a second car conveying Indira, and Melissa from Acquisitions. Indira had Jay's charm-book on hand, its secrets now fully in her control courtesy of Orlando. Melissa is something of an expert in what we shall give the civilised name of *infiltration*. No concealment spells can long stand up to *her*.

Milady was as supportive of our immediate departure as I could wish, though she did ask one or two inconvenient questions.

'What will you do once you locate the castle?'

'Something fiendishly clever and more than a little heroic.'

'Please answer more sensibly, Ves. This is serious.'

'I *know* that. I have no answer to make. I don't know what we'll do when we get there; it's my job, and Rob's, to figure that out. Which is a more petrifying prospect today than it has ever been before.'

'I have no doubt you are both fully equal to the challenge.'

'Thank you. Are you sure it is wise to take Indira?'

'No, but she appears to have the knack of locating her brother.'

'Melissa could do that.'

'Probably, but it would take time to make over that duty to her, and were you not desirous of an instant departure?'

'Yes...'

'What's more, Indira begged hard to be included.'

'Forgive me, ma'am, but you are not always so receptive to pleas.'

'What would you do if I forbade you to go?'

'Go anyway.'

'Mm. Indira has not quite the same level of resolve, but until her brother is retrieved she will not have a moment's peace.'

'Very kind of you, Milady.'

'Besides that, I am interested to see how she does in the field. The question of her future with the Society is not yet fully decided.'

That's Milady for you: kindness wrapped in ruthless practicality, or maybe the other way around.

I suppose it's necessary if you are in command of two hundred people.

I made no further objection, only hoping in private that I would not manage to lose shy, tremulous Indira the same way I'd mislaid her brother. If I did, Jay wouldn't even have to kill me; I'd save him the trouble and immolate myself.

Focus, Ves. Act now, panic later.

We made the trip in under two hours, though it was difficult to know exactly when we had arrived. We drove through Sutton Weaver and out the other side, then performed a rough circle around it through a series of narrow, bumpy little roads. No castle appeared on the horizon to enliven the expense of green, flat fields.

Not a surprise, but not helpful either.

Rob dialled. 'Mel,' he said to his phone. 'Needing a better plan.' He listened for a minute, then shut it off. 'Pull over somewhere,' he said to me. 'We're on foot for the rest.'

I found a spot by the side of the road that seemed safe enough, and pulled my car as far over into the grassy verge as I dared (blessing my choice of a Countryman all the while). Out we got. Neither Mel nor Indira paused at all; they conferred briefly together, then set off into the field, leaving Rob and me to follow them.

If anything, Indira seemed to be leading the way. She had Jay's location to work from, I supposed, which at least gave her a direction to head in. It would be down to Melissa to —

— well, for example, to wave a magick Wand and make a castle appear. Which she did.

I've oversimplified the process a little, to be sure. She certainly took up her Wand — a sparkling amethyst specimen I have occasionally eyed myself — but she did not flourish it about. She merely tapped it against her lip in a gesture more thoughtful than flamboyant, and *bits* of a castle rippled into view: a section of brown brick wall with a heavy timber door, and a glimpse of a moat.

The vision wavered like water, and vanished again.

'Oh, yes,' said Melissa, as though she had mislaid her keys and happened to come across them again. 'There it is.' She proceeded to do a bit of Wand-waving, but in an odd, graceless way: she poked at the air before her as though sticking pins in something, and then began to jab and slash. With each gesture more of the castle appeared; Melissa was tearing away the illusions which concealed it, like a dressmaker armed with a stout pair of scissors.

At length, the whole building was revealed: a fanciful structure despite the plain brown bricks, all sloping roofs and arched windows, its various wings and annexes piled higgledy-piggledy against one another. It was unusually large, but I spied at least one section which looked as though it had been added sometime after the castle's original construction.

'Jay is this way,' said Indira, and pointed. She indicated a corner of the castle which boasted a splendid fairytale tower, round-walled, with a conical roof and a single long, arched window. Was Jay at the top? I made a mental note to be ready with sleeping beauty jokes, which could not fail to endear me to Jay.

We advanced, veering a little left in the direction of that corner turret.

I found this puzzling. Melissa and Indira seemed intent upon simply walking openly into Ashdown Castle, picking up Jay and Bill and (presumably) walking out again.

'Er,' I said after half a minute. 'Should we not... I don't know, *skulk* or something?'

'I want to attract some attention,' said Melissa.

'Um. Why?'

'Because in about twelve seconds, Rob and I will kick up a ruckus while you and Indira *skulk* into the castle and heroically extract Jay.'

'Couldn't we have talked about this before?'

'I've only just decided it.'

I swallowed my irritation, which flared up all the more at the words *I've decided*. Who appointed Melissa Supreme Leader of our expedition anyway?! But since I could come up with no better plan, it did not behove me to complain.

Instead, I wielded my lovely spangled Sunstone Wand and wove some concealment charms of my own, first around myself and then around Indira. By the time I had finished, anyone glancing only cursorily at the spot I was standing in would see nothing; I'd made of myself a wisp of breeze, and Indira was an errant ray of sunlight.

Not a moment too soon, either, for about two minutes later a palpable shock rippled through the floor and pulsed in the air before us; we had hit the castle's next layer of defence, a magickal field which repelled anyone not authorised to enter. We had exactly the same kind of thing set up at Home.

It is not easy to pass such a structure, but with a pair of Wands at our disposal, Melissa and I were well prepared. My Sunstone buzzed with magick; I tapped the tip of the Wand against Melissa's and the power doubled. We turned them upon the repelling field before us and burned away a fair-sized hole. A warm wind billowed through from the other side.

'Go,' said Melissa tersely.

I went first, glancing back just once to see Rob standing poised a few feet behind me, legs braced, chin lifted: ready for anything.

I didn't like to leave him or Melissa to take the heat for us, but it would not be fair of me to doubt their ability to deal with it. I hopped through the hole we'd made, pulling Indira after me — and almost died of fright to find Katalin Pataki and George Mercer not ten feet away from us.

11

I TENSED, TRYING TO keep Indira behind me while I kept a close watch on the two Ancestria Magicka agents. Would they spot us? Melissa's plan of serving as decoy had been put to an unexpectedly early test.

They did not. Something caught Mercer's attention; his eyes shifted briefly in our direction, and a faint frown flitted across his face. But Melissa spoke up just then, and his attention returned to her.

'Hi,' she said. 'So we know that, officially, you had nothing to do with the disappearance of Jay Patel and the book he found at Farringale. But unofficially, we all know that's rubbish. We come to offer a bargain. Keep the book. Return Jay.'

Katalin smiled. 'And if Mr. Patel does not wish to return to the Society?'

Mercer said, at the same time, 'You propose to do what to us, exactly, if we do not agree?'

They needed a lesson or two in negotiation, I thought privately. Typically it would be more productive to pursue only one line of argument at a time; two would confuse the issue and weaken the impact of both. But perhaps they had not been working together long.

Lucky that I had often had cause to test my concealment charms before. I know them to be virtually foolproof. I walked nonchalantly past Pataki and Mercer, drawing Indira with me. She looked far more concerned by the situation than I felt; she crept past them, oh-so-carefully, casting frequent nervous glances in their direction. I tried to reassure her by patting her on the arm, but I do not think my gesture was much heeded.

She relaxed a bit once we were safely past, and had covered a distance of some thirty feet or so. We were rapidly drawing up to the castle by then, and I was engaged in searching for the nearest and most convenient way in.

Indira gave a tiny sigh of relief.

'We were in no danger,' I told her.

'No danger? We were practically standing on their toes!'

'No danger whatsoever.'

Indira frowned. 'What did she mean about Jay's not wanting to return to us?'

'She was trying to manipulate Melissa, that's all. Obviously they would like to keep both Jay and the book, and without our making too much trouble for them over either.'

'I don't think they can care all that much about our making trouble. This seems like an obvious challenge to the Society.'

'Not quite, as they've officially denied it from the beginning. It's a gambit, a throw of the dice to see what happens. It isn't a declaration of war, yet.'

'Yet?'

'That will probably come in time.' We were prowling around the base of the turret by that time, and I'd spied a way in.

Good points: the door was not barred or padlocked and a cautious probe of its magickal defences revealed nothing I did not feel able to handle with the help of my spangled Wand.

Bad points: Historic buildings have a way of being odd, whimsical and downright contrary sometimes, and this one was a prime example. There was a door in the tower, but it was inexplicably situated halfway up the building. There were no stairs leading up to it, nor any sign that there had ever been any.

'Hm,' I said. I wished for a second that I had brought my Chair with me. I, like everyone else, have a flying specimen;

Val and I had both gone for tall, wing-backed chairs with comfortably padded seats, high-rising armrests and plush velvet upholstery. Hers is in green, mine's burgundy. With my Chair, we could whizz up to the door in no time; in fact we could go all the way up to the window, and skip the door entirely.

Of course, I would have had to travel the entire distance by Chair, for there's no way I could ever fit it in my Mini. And two hours by Chair in uncertain April weather is nobody's idea of a good time. Not now that there are cars.

So, no Chair. We would have to do it the tiring way.

'How far has your education progressed?' I asked Indira.

'My magickal education? Um, the... the usual?' She looked at me uncertainly.

'More specifically, can you levitate?'

'Oh! Yes.' Indira proved this by instantly levitating herself up to a distance of about two feet from the ground, smiling at me in that hopeful, shy way she has, like a puppy wishing for praise.

'Er,' I said. 'Yes, that's very good.' It was more than good. Levitation is one of the more difficult arts; some otherwise very powerful magickers at the Society cannot manage it at all. Even one such as yours truly, among the finer practitioners of levitation at Home, can do it only with difficulty, and I have never managed to levitate myself more than about ten feet up without serious strain.

Indira levitated in the same way she breathed: effortlessly. And she hovered there, two feet up, with no visible sign that she was tiring at all. She looked like she could sail up ten feet and more still with similar ease, and I suppressed just the faintest, unworthy tinge of jealousy.

She will be the best of us, Jay had said, and I could see what he meant.

I took a deep breath.

'Right,' I said decisively. 'We're going to levitate to the door.' Which, happily, looked to be only eight or nine feet up; I might manage to accomplish the business without embarrassing myself. 'I will take care of its defences and then we'll go in and get Jay. He's still in there?'

Indira nodded. 'Probably in the top— oh, no. Wait a moment.' She frowned and consulted her book of Jay's charms again. 'He's moved a bit, he's— oh! He's coming down.'

The door swung open above our heads, and Jay appeared. 'Hi,' he said, and then dropped down to land beside us with the grace of a panther.

I eyed him with some displeasure. 'Hi? That's it?'

'Hail, fair rescuers,' Jay said, with a smile for me. 'I am full honoured by your braving the dangers of Ashdown in order to retrieve me... oh, wait. You *are* here for me? You aren't just here for the book?'

I waited for him to explode at me over Indira's presence, but he greeted her with a swift peck on the cheek and a brotherly pat of approval, and showed no signs of displeasure.

I felt, once again, that I had not quite got the measure of Jay.

'We're here for both,' I said, and Jay made a show of wiping his brow in relief. 'Do you have the book?'

'No, but I know where it is. Come on.' Jay led the way around the turret and on, presumably leading us to some other entrance. Mindful of threats and bristling with caution, Indira and I followed.

Indira put Jay's charm book into her brother's hand, and he tucked it away with a smile of thanks. 'I knew you'd figure that out,' he told her.

She gave that shy smile. 'How did you know we were here?'

'Because Ves shines like a bloody beacon.'

I blanched. 'Er. I do?'

'Yes, but don't worry. Anyone who didn't know you would just think that a small sun had popped by for a visit.'

'Reassuring.' I wasted a little time trying to decide what Jay meant, exactly; it's never been mentioned before. But probably it had something to do with my being unusually, er, *amplified* by the Sunstone Wand, and anyway, the more important question was: had Pataki and Mercer observed the same thing, and pretended not to notice?

'We might want to be careful, then,' I said. 'They probably know we are here.' I wrestled with the Wand a bit, hopeful of diminishing my beacon-ness by a shade or two.

Jay dampened me with a wave of his hand. I don't know how to describe it other than to say that; I felt quenched, like he had thrown a bucket of water over me. Then I understood what he had meant: I had been positively ablaze with magick, and had not even noticed.

'Were you angry, by chance?' Jay said to me.

'Of course I was angry! They thieved Bill and kidnapped you!'

'They certainly did thieve Bill, which was disgraceful and nothing can exonerate them from that piece of infamy. But they did not kidnap me, precisely.'

'They didn't?'

'They offered me a job.'

I blinked. 'And?'

'And I accepted.'

Indira gasped. I stifled an impulse to kick him somewhere painful.

Jay laughed. 'Only temporarily. What better way to get a look around their HQ than to walk in here as a new recruit? And I wanted a shot at getting Bill back.'

'So they just let you walk in here?'

'Sort of. I've been under close supervision, and they have as yet withheld all privileges.'

I looked around. 'You are remarkably alone for a man under close supervision.'

'Well, when I saw you two on the approach I knew it was time to end the charade. I ditched my supervisor and broke out of the tower.'

Indira clutched at her brother's arm, probably experiencing feelings of knee-weakening relief.

I was experiencing feelings more like incandescent rage.

'You're blazing again, Ves,' said Jay, and I again had to suffer the quenching sensation. It is not especially pleasant.

'I would not blaze if you wouldn't keep making me angry,' I said tightly.

He stopped, and looked at me in genuine surprise. 'How did I do that?'

I controlled myself with an effort. 'You let us imagine you kidnapped.'

'I thought you would realise what I was up to.'

'How was I supposed to realise that?!'

'Um.' Jay looked at his sister. 'Right. I see. I'm sorry.'

Indira looked at the floor.

I took a slow breath, and let go of my need to punch him. Not without some regret. 'Another time, could you possibly get word to me about your wily plans?'

'I can try. I didn't have a phone, of course, and nobody would let me borrow one for some reason.'

'*For some reason.* Are you sure they believed your show of willingness to jump ships?'

'I don't see why not.' Jay began walking again. 'They asked me what the Society was paying me, then offered me ten times that.'

'*TEN TIMES?*'

Jay cast me a look of mild irritation. 'Yes, if we are going to engage in any kind of stealth mission here you're going to need to *stop with the blazing.*'

Ten times. For goodness' sake! The Society paid its staff as well as it could afford to, and if Jay's salary was anything like mine (and it would be, considering his Waymaster-ness) then he was by no means hard done to. Ten times more! Who could afford that?

I felt a faint twinge of nerves. 'Er. You do actually intend to turn that down, right?'

Jay rolled his eyes. 'Obviously.'

'Obviously? Not many people would say no to that kind of money.'

'I think you are doing "people" an injustice, but since I at least am not overburdened with avarice I think we can all stop worrying about that. Ah.' Jay stopped before an apparently featureless patch of brick wall, and stared at it with palpable satisfaction. 'Here we go.' He spoke a word

I did not understand, and one of the bricks glowed. He touched his fingers to the shiny brick, and the wall fell away.

'Secret passwords?' I said in disgust. 'Really?'

Jay grinned. 'These people are a bit old-school.' He led the way through the not-wall, while Indira followed and I brought up the rear.

'The irony of hearing the words *old school* uttered with such derision by a member of the Society for Magickal Heritage.'

'Fair. Perhaps I meant staggeringly cliché, but I'm not complaining. My sojourn into espionage has borne fruit.' He stopped talking and stopped walking at the same time, though we had not yet proceeded far into the castle. The door-in-the-wall had brought us, incongruously, into a muddy boot-room wherein many pairs of Wellingtons and assorted hiking boots were littered about. Beyond that was the kind of chilly, bleak hallway to be found in the servants' quarters of any house of at least moderate size that saw use during the Victorian period. Jay stopped us before the typical green baize-covered door, the more or less soundproof kind that muffle all those undesirable noises that emanate from the service parts of the house. Perfectly insufferable to have to listen to the clamour of one's dinner being cooked, isn't it?

Only this one was not quite soundproof, because I could hear something coming from the other side. Someone was singing.

If you intend thus to disdain,
It does the more enrapture me,
And even so, I still remain
A lover in captivity.

The melody was familiar, and so was the voice.

'Why,' I whispered to Jay, 'is Bill singing Greensleeves?'

'Er.' Cautiously, Jay pulled open the door an inch or so. The song immediately swelled in volume, as Bill launched full-throated into the chorus.

Greensleeves was all my joy!
Greensleeves was my delight!
Greensleeves was my heart of gold!
And who but my lady greensleeves!

'Were you wearing green yesterday?' Jay murmured.

'With pink hair? Don't be ridiculous.'

Jay swung the door open. Considering this decision I expected to find the room beyond empty except for Bill, but it was not.

We'd come out in what looked to be a tiny library, though the chamber was barely larger than the boot-room. The walls were crowded with bookcases fitted edge-to-edge, each crammed full of books. Bill lay enthroned in splendour upon a central table, open to display one of John Wester's journal pages.

Seated before him and wearing a long-suffering expression was the kind of cardi-clad middle-aged lady you might expect to see serving dinner at a school cafeteria, or perhaps selling raffle tickets at a Women's Institute fundraising drive. Whatever instant (and doubtless unfair) judgements one might make about such a person, the last thing *I* expected was that she would detect the sounds of Jay's approach almost before it seemed possible, be out of her chair and facing us in about two seconds flat, and hurling hexes at us with the help of a pretty jade Wand.

12

SOMEHOW, THE PATELS WERE ready for this. Indira had a very good, very stout shield charm up in no time, which absorbed the first wave of the indignant woman's hexery. Jay meanwhile threw a hex of his own in response, a neat, clever piece of magick which would have knocked her out on the spot if it had hit her. Sadly, she proved to have remarkable reflexes, too, and ducked.

Through all of this ruckus, Bill warbled on.

'Come on, Amelia,' said Jay, throwing another hex. 'You know the book isn't yours.'

She made no reply to this, choosing to focus all her attention on the next wave of dark curses.

Hm.

I plucked a sleep-bead from one of my emergency supplies pockets. No use expecting to get her to swallow it; not with hexes, reflexes and a Wand at her disposal. Instead I threw the bead up, blasted it with a shot of energy from my own spangly Wand, and watched in satisfaction as it sprayed the curse-happy woman in the most potent sleep potion our technicians are capable of brewing.

The woman uttered a word I shall not repeat here, cast me a look of utter hatred, and dropped like a stone.

'I need some of those,' said Jay.

Greensleeves was all my joy! sang Bill.

I went over to him at once and patted his pages. 'Bill.'

Greensleeves was my delight!

'Bill! Stop!'

Bill stopped. 'Miss Vesper?'

'The same. We are about to effect your rescue, and it would be preferable if you were a bit quieter. Early modern love songs might be delightful but they do attract more notice than would be desirable.'

'I cannot begin to express the extent of my gratitude,' said Bill. 'I shall consider myself under an obligation to you for the rest of my natural life.'

How long is a book's natural life? Probably much longer than mine. 'You don't like Ancestria Magicka, I take it?'

'If you are referring to these scoundrels who have wrested me from you, then your surmise is correct.'

They did not appear to have mistreated Bill, in fairness to them. He lay atop a particularly plush cushion, his spine perfectly supported. He had an entire table to himself, and they had let him go on singing to his heart's content (though that might have been because he would not oblige them so far as to shut up). He had not been damaged, as far as I could see.

I thought it interesting, and possibly significant, that the woman I had felled had apparently been studying John Wester's journal entries when we had come in. In all the excitement about Bill's unusual composition, we had rather overlooked the contents of his pages; what were they but the ramblings of a robber and a thief? But if Ancestria Magicka thought differently, then I wanted to know why. I busied myself snapping pictures of each of Bill's pages that bore writing (except for Zareen's section). These I sent through to Val. I sent a note with them: *Decipher?*

Then I scooped up Bill.

'It is good to be with you again,' said Bill, which was sweet of him.

'Sometime you'll have to tell me who Milady Greensleeves is,' I said.

During my hasty camera-session with Bill, Indira had busied herself with searching the outer garments of the sleeping woman. Jay snatched up the notebook she had left upon the table, and leafed speedily through it. He showed me something interesting: Amelia had made an ink sketch of the map at the back of Bill's pages, with annotations.

'Hang onto that,' I said.

'Mm.' Jay pocketed it. There were two doors in the room: one leading back the way we had come, the other to who-knew-where-else. Retracing our steps was the obvious solution if we wanted to get out, and Jay clearly agreed, for he made for the door at speed. But before he reached it, there came the sounds of heavy footsteps approaching from the other side. 'Uh oh,' said Jay, pivoted, and dashed for the other door at a run.

Indira got there before him. She tugged mightily upon the door but to her chagrin, it did not budge. 'Locked,' she reported.

Well, no surprise there. They had stashed the most valuable book in the world in this tiny library, with only Amelia to look after it; they were hardly going to leave the main door unlocked.

The other door swung open to reveal George Mercer, and Katalin Pataki right behind him.

'See,' said Mercer with grim satisfaction. 'I knew he was full of shit.' He had the air and the accent of a public school boy, and the clothes to match. I wondered which of our most respected establishments had been responsible for turning out such a fine specimen.

Katalin regarded Jay with some disappointment, though she said, in her thick Hungarian accent: 'Is he, though? Let me have the book, Jay.'

'That is Mr. Patel to you,' said Bill.

Jay grinned, and backed up until he was shoulder-to-shoulder with Indira and me. He took Bill from me, probably in order to leave my hands free to wield my Wand.

Katalin, though, interpreted his actions differently. 'Good,' she purred. 'Mr. Patel has more sense than to imagine us as the enemy. Our goals are the same, are they not?'

'As what?' I demanded. 'The Society doesn't steal.'

'We stole nothing. Upon learning that an active Waymaster happened to be the current keeper of a remarkable book, we naturally approached him with an attractive offer of employment. One which he would be a fool to turn down.' Katalin smiled at Jay.

'It is not my book, of course,' said Jay. 'If anyone can claim right of ownership over it, that would be the Troll Court.'

Katalin's smile widened. 'Finders, keepers,' she purred.

My mind travelled back over all the Treasures, Curiosities, rare books and other artefacts I had tracked down and rescued from destruction over my decade with the Society. Finders, keepers? 'Oh, if *only!* I would be filthy rich by now, and retiring to my own island.'

'About that,' said Mercer. 'We're instructed to extend a similarly lucrative offer to Specialists Cordelia Vesper and Indira Patel.' He waved a document at me, as though that might convince me if his words did not. 'Ancestria Magicka is in need of people with your unique talents.'

Indira looked flabbergasted.

I felt a twinge of curiosity. 'Are you?' I murmured. 'Instructed by whom?'

Mercer's mouth twitched with annoyance. 'You will meet your new employers once you have accepted their generous offer.'

'Like Jay has?'

Mercer looked Jay over expressionlessly. 'Mr. Patel's actions have delivered not only a Waymaster and the book to our Castle but a highly experienced acquisitions specialist and one of the most promising spellwrights the University has ever encountered. Our organisation is very pleased with him.'

All of this was sounding horribly like they had no intention of allowing us to turn down their offer. 'We do have a choice, I suppose?' I said acidly.

'Of course,' said Mercer, and gave me a polite, insincere smile. 'You will find us to be perfectly civilised. Regrettably, however, it will not be in our power to permit you to leave Ashdown with the book in your possession.'

'Think about it, Ves,' said Katalin, and I blinked at her in surprise at her use of my nickname. 'Ten times the salary, ten times the freedom! We are sent all over the world, to the farthest corners of the globe. We have already retrieved ancient Treasures the likes of which you have never seen.'

I admit, I experienced a faint twinge of wistful desire at this picture of well-salaried freedom. But the feeling did not last long. 'All of which you directly repatriated to their home countries, of course?' I said.

Katalin's mouth set into a hard line of disappointment. 'You are wasted on the Society.'

'It may be something of a raggle-taggle organisation,' I admitted, 'without the resources to pay island-purchasing salaries, and I cannot deny that I am sometimes chafed by Milady's rules. But the work we do is far more important than you will ever understand.'

Katalin shrugged, and looked at Indira.

I wondered what the poor girl would manage to say under such pressure as that; even small-talking with her new colleagues at the Society's cafeteria often left her tongue-tied.

But I underestimated her. She might only have been able to utter one word, but it was the right word, and spoken with a conviction which must preclude all argument. 'No,' she said.

Katalin sighed. 'I suppose that means you will be leaving us too, Mr. Patel?'

'Correct.'

'The book, then, please.' She held out her hands to receive it.

Jay only gripped it tighter. 'I'm afraid not.'

Katalin and George Mercer exchanged the kind of grim glance that had to mean big trouble for the three of us. Fortunately, we were all at that moment distracted by the terrific sound of crashing glass that might, for example, be indicative of a window breaking.

'Ah,' said Rob, peering in through the ragged hole where there had, only a moment ago, been big, bright panes of glass. I caught a glimpse of Melissa standing just behind him.

Excellent.

'Indira. Chairs,' I said, already making for the nearest one to me. I did not have time to explain, and could only hope that she would grasp my meaning.

See, Rob and I have been out on quite a few missions together before. There was this one time, several years ago now, where he and I got into a pretty difficult situation. There was Rob, there was me, there was a locked room halfway up an unreasonably tall building, and there was a rabid ogre. Enough said? But Rob had put his hand to the glass and pulled one of his fabulously destructive tricks; the entire window turned black-as-night and fell outwards, and when I had witched us up a couple of Chairs we flew serenely away into the sunset.

I never did find out what became of the ogre.

The timing had been slightly tighter before, but then, I had not had the Wand. This time it was the work of a few seconds to persuade my chosen chair — a fairly comfy, tapestry-clad armchair type thing — that it was livelier in nature than it had ever before imagined itself to be, and might rather enjoy taking flight. Indira, to my relief (if not much to my surprise) caught on right away, and made short work of an engraved oak desk chair until it actually began to dance on its four rigid legs.

We witched up three more, during which time Katalin Pataki was unwise enough to make an advance upon Rob and Melissa, while George tried to wrench Bill from Jay. The latter encounter ended with Jay shoving the book through the window into Melissa's hands — a risky manoeuvre, which very nearly resulted in Katalin's swiping it on the spot — and then (to my exasperation) he abandoned magick altogether in favour of fisticuffs.

I did not linger to watch the two men swing at each other. I pointed my Wand in Katalin's direction. It was unfair, really; she was facing Rob and Melissa, and too engaged in opposing their joint attacks to have any leisure to attend to me. I shot a binding charm at her, nicely amplified by the power of the Sunstone Wand, and she collapsed in a motionless heap. Almost motionless. She was twitching a bit.

I assuaged my slightly guilty conscience by remembering how very unscrupulous most of her organisation's activities had thus far been, and shoved her out of the way of the window. 'Sorry,' I said brightly, ignoring the way her eyes blazed hatred in my general direction. 'But I can't let you have Bill. We've grown fond of each other.'

I bundled Indira out of the window next, desk chair and all. She shot into the sky beyond, clutching the side of her Chair with her one good arm, and almost as rigid with fright as Katalin was with magick. I made a note to send her to the infirmary once we got home; she might be in need of a little therapy.

Melissa went next in my fine tapestry Chair, taking Bill with her. Good.

As one, Rob and I turned to Jay.

He wasn't doing badly, to be fair to him. Not badly at all. His face displayed the evidence of George Mercer's talents at fisticuffs, and he had obviously taken more than one hit judging from the damage. But Mercer was little better off, and I admit to taking some small satisfaction at the mess Jay had made both of his artlessly tumbled curls and his coolly self-possessed demeanour.

Nonetheless, it was high time to cut in. Rob — taking advantage of Mercer's distraction in much the same shameless way I had taken advantage of Katalin's — felled our public school tosser with a solid punch to the jaw, while I shoved a Chair under Jay's legs until he toppled into it. I sent him out the window with a flick of the Wand.

With a startled yelp and what might have been a vicious curse upon my ancestors, he disappeared.

Rob and I followed.

Flying by Chair is quite the experience, and it's really something to do it as part of a small flock. I lounged back at my ease, much better off than poor Indira, for my chosen vehicle had a wide seat and tall arms to keep me from falling out. But it was her first time; she would soon develop a better eye for this kind of thing. And she had got herself out of the library speedily, efficiently and successfully. I was very pleased with her.

Melissa, I noted, had caught up, and steadied Indira with a firm grip on the back of her Chair. She was in no danger of falling off, injured arm notwithstanding; good.

I steered clear of Jay, at least until we made it back to our abandoned cars. He had a fine brooding-glower-of-displeasure going on which I did not wish to tangle with.

He opted to ride with Indira.

I opted to attribute this to a positive cause, like brotherly concern rather than Ves-avoidance.

We made it back to our cars unpursued, piled hastily into them and drove away, Bill in such fine fettle that he began singing again. The strains of *Greensleeves* hung dulcet upon the air, fading into silence as Melissa's car pulled out ahead of us.

We had to leave the Chairs behind, of course, and I do wonder a little what might have become of our escape-pods. I would like to apologise right now to any dog-walker or jogger who might have been puzzled to discover a cluster of library chairs abandoned on the edge of a field, apparently a long way from anywhere. I promise, the explanation is perfectly reasonable.

13

By the time we arrived back at Home, Jay still had not quite forgiven me for bundling him out of Ashdown library like a sack of clothes. He was waiting for me in the hall, cool as a marble statue, with Indira at his elbow and no sign of Melissa.

'Hello,' I said, with a hopeful smile. I cannot absolutely confirm that I did not employ surreptitious use of the puppy eyes, too.

'We need to see Milady right away,' said Jay, unmoved.

'I did not, by my interference, mean any slight upon your very excellent abilities.'

'I was fine.'

I tried not to stare too obviously at the bruises on his face. 'I know!'

Apparently I failed, for the brow came down in annoyance and he involuntarily touched the biggest of the bruises: a great monster of a thing adorning his right cheek. 'No one's ever died of a little bruise.'

'I mean... I'm not a doctor, but that probably isn't true.'

I thought I saw the corner of Jay's mouth twitch, but I was probably mistaken. 'Shall we go?' said he, and gestured for me to precede him up the main stairs.

Desperate times, desperate measures. 'How many ways, can I say sorry...' I said melodically, drawing out the last word.

'Is that... are you using Phil Collins against me?' It wasn't his mouth that was twitching this time; there was a definite spasm going on in his left eye.

'Who can resist Phil!'

'One or two people,' muttered Indira, though when I looked at her she tried her best to outdo her brother's statue impression.

'So,' said Jay meaningfully, and pointed in the direction of Milady's tower: up. 'Heaven's that way.'

I sang about paradise, sashaying up the stairs.

'It can't be heaven *and* paradise up there,' said Jay. 'Pick one.'

'I say both.'

'You're just hoping for a promotion.'

'I was recently offered a rather tempting job opportunity, which I very loyally turned down. A raise isn't too much to hope for, is it?'

'Wretch.' I may not have been able to see Jay anymore, having smartly turned my back upon him. I could, however, hear the smile.

Hah.

'Bill!' I called. 'I have no doubt that you and Milady will be delighted with one another.'

'I shall be happy to make the acquaintance of so esteemed a person,' Bill replied 'Her ladyship...?' Bill trailed off into an expectant pause.

'Yes,' said Jay.

'Her ladyship of which family?'

Bill, bless him, was labouring under the impression that Milady had a name. Or that any of us might know what it is.

'Just Milady, Bill,' I called, as Jay floundered for a response.

'Milady is a title, not a name.'

'In this case, it is both.'

Bill was silent, either with indignation or with shock, I couldn't tell which.

'Welcome back, Jay,' said Milady when we reached her tower room. The air sparkled with a special brilliance which usually meant that her ladyship was extra pleased.

That of course meant that she had been extra worried, even if she had shown little sign of it before.

'Thank you, Milady,' said Jay with a bow. 'It is good to be back.'

'Indira rocked it,' I announced, making the poor girl blush.

'Did she? I cannot say I am surprised.'

'And Jay was not kidnapped at all, the wretch.'

Silence. There was a quality to the air that suggested Milady's eyebrows might have been raised a little high, had she corporeal presence enough to display it.

Jay rolled his eyes at me. 'May I explain?'

'Pray do.'

He explained. I did not find his reasons any more satisfactory than last time, though to his credit he only made himself out to be *somewhat* stupendously the hero. He accepted Milady's admonishments — rather milder than mine — with reasonable grace.

Then Milady ruined everything by saying: 'That was very clever, Jay. Good work.'

Jay smirked at me. I considered it only fair to respond by sticking out my tongue at him.

Indira watched this exchange with wide, wide eyes.

We followed this by apprising Milady of everything that had happened since our urgent departure for Ashdown Castle, a discussion that proceeded at some length. At long last, Bill made himself known by shuffling his covers in irritation, wafting dust everywhere.

'Where have you been keeping that?' I said to him in astonishment. He'd spent several hours in Val's care, and ought therefore to have emerged spotlessly dust-free.

'I reserve a small supply in case it should prove necessary,' said Bill loftily.

'Displeasure registered.'

'Thank you.'

I made introductions, which was an awkward business considering it was between an unusually loquacious book and an unusually disembodied voice. Bill, to my disgust, turned on the charm so much that I suspected him of snobbery.

Jay passed Amelia's notebook to me. It was open at the page with her ink-drawing of the map. 'There's something odd about them,' he said, interrupting Bill's compliments upon the unusual beauty of Milady's rich, heavenly voice (his words, not mine). It occurred to me to marvel a moment at the transformation: that we (or Zareen) should have succeeded in turning a foul-mouthed wretch of a book into a silver-tongued charmer. Behold, the power of literature.

'In which particular respect?' said Milady.

Jay paused a moment to gather his thoughts. 'Amelia spent a long time with Bill,' he began. 'Studying him, probably, at least at first. But she spent a lot more time talking to him.'

'Impertinent woman,' muttered Bill.

Jay smiled faintly. 'Or trying to, as Bill flatly refused to talk to anyone but me or Ves. So, they pulled me off supervising the construction of their new henge, and—'

'A new *henge*?' interrupted Milady.

Apparently we had forgotten to tell her about Milton Keynes. 'At the top of a tower,' said Jay. 'Breeze blocks. Ugly in the extreme, but functional enough.'

I almost dropped the notebook. 'They're making a henge out of *concrete*?'

'I'm afraid so.'

'Have they no soul?'

'Not a scrap between them. Anyway, they had me interrogating Bill on Amelia's behalf for more than half the day, and she chose a strange line of enquiry. I expected the kinds of questions our lot were asking — burning historical questions no one has ever found the answer to; details about his life and history; the nature of the enchantments that made him; that sort of thing. But all Amelia wanted to know about was his creator, and where she is buried.'

'I see,' said Milady. 'And what is known about this person that might account for so extraordinary a display of interest?'

'Nowhere near enough. Even Bill's information could not satisfy Amelia, exactly.'

'I was unable to give information about the precise location of my former mistress's grave,' Bill put in. 'On account of not having been chosen to be present at her burial.'

I eyed the map in Amelia's notebook. Her annotations were difficult to read, but they looked like place names, sometimes scrawled with a question mark beside them. The map itself wasn't very helpful, not even the original; it had no distinct features about it, no labels, no directions. It consisted only of a few hastily-inked lines which might have related to virtually anything — roads, hills, rivers...

'It may seem obvious,' I began apologetically, 'but did you ask Amelia why she wanted to know about Bill's former mistress?'

'I did, as nonchalantly as I could. She just looked at me like she couldn't believe I would ask such a stupid question, like the answer should have been perfectly obvious.'

I sighed. 'Any guesses, Bill?'

'I know nothing of my mistress that might explain this unseemly interest in the manner or location of her demise.'

John Wester, whoever he was, had been peculiarly absorbed by the search for Drogryre's grave. Ancestria Magicka, centuries later, were intent upon following in his footsteps — indeed, by Jay's account they were more interested in that question than they were in anything else Bill had to offer. Which, considering the utterly remarkable nature of him, was extraordinary. What did they expect to find in Drogryre's grave that was of greater value than Bill himself?

'Do you know where she died?' I asked him.

'Lavenham. That is the town in which we had taken up residence when she became ill, and quickly died.'

'Of the plague.'

'The sweating sickness.'

My ears pricked up a bit at that, which may sound macabre but many a historian would react the same way. The sweating sickness was a strange form of plague which cropped up out of nowhere in about 1485 and vanished some sixty or so years later, never to be heard of again. More oddly still, it was confined to England for some years, and only belatedly spread into Ireland and Europe. It's still sometimes referred to as the "English Sweat". No theory as to its possible causes can account for all of its recorded symptoms.

And the best part of all, *of all*, is this: the very first symptom of having contracted this plague consisted of an overpowering sense of dread. In other words, one felt one's doom rapidly approaching.

I realise I sound like Zareen, but how fabulously weird is all of that?

Of course, all things considered (especially that last part) it is highly likely that the sweating sickness was of magickal origin. While it is fair to say that the historians of the non-magickal world are a shade more confused about it all than we are, it is also fair to note that none of *us* has ever yet managed to uncover the plague's original author either.

'Bill!' I said. 'What was the cause of the sweating sickness?'

'I have no information on that topic.'

It was worth a try.

So, Drogryre rocked the magickal world back in the fifteenth century, produced a feat of such remarkable power as Bill, but somehow never achieved any prominent position within magickal history in spite of this — perhaps because she died of the sweat soon afterwards.

Or perhaps not.

'I need to talk to Zareen,' I said.

'An excellent notion. Go at once,' said Milady. 'There'll be chocolate in the pot.'

THERE WAS, TOO, THOUGH it took a few moments to spot it in the midst of Zareen's clutter. One of Milady's favourite eighteenth-century tea pots, an elegant silver specimen, stood at one corner of the desk, its tall spout steaming in a promising fashion.

Zareen lounged in her chair, booted feet on the desk as usual. She had one smallish ancient-looking book in her hands and about seven more stacked in front of her. When she saw me, she set down her book and adjusted her posture to a more respectable configuration — sweeping the pot onto the floor in the process.

I caught it with a flick of a finger, and carefully floated it back up to the table-top. 'Don't waste the chocolate!' I chided.

'Never,' said Zareen fervently. Milady had thoughtfully provided two cups — two, because Jay and Indira had taken themselves off someplace else. To my regret they had escorted Bill along with them, though no one had seemed very interested in explaining to me where they were going or what they proposed to do with the book.

I tried not to feel hurt.

Zareen and I fell upon the chocolate (not literally). I was feeling strained and tired after such a long, chaotic, stressful day, and guzzled my restorative chocolate more quickly than could ever be called ladylike. I felt better.

This done, I caught Zareen up on recent developments. Her eyes, like mine, brightened at the words "sweating sickness". We are a peculiar bunch, aren't we? 'So Drogryre was part of the first wave of the sweat,' Zareen mused when I had finished. 'One of the very first to die.'

'Seems so.'

'Hmm.'

'Do you suppose that has anything to do with this unseemly eagerness to dig her up again?'

'I don't see how, but you never know.'

I dismissed this with a wave. A careful one, since I was on my second cup of chocolate. 'Questions! What's so special about Drogryre? Why haven't we heard of her, when she seems to have been absurdly powerful and pretty clever besides? How have *they* heard of her, and what's the interest in her place of rest? And who the hell is John Wester? — Oh! Wester. Right.' I'd forgotten I had sent the pages over to Val, nor had I checked since for a response. I did that.

There was a string of messages from Val.

Ves, said the first one. *Much as I applaud your initiative, you're an idiot if you think I hadn't taken copies of my own the moment I got your precious book into my sticky little hands.*

Well, that was fair.

Idiosyncratic use of English, said the next one. *Generally classifiable as Late Middle English, but eccentric enough in spelling, grammar etc to suggest Wester wasn't far from being illiterate. Wondering therefore why he purloined Bill at all, and what motive he had for writing any of his adventures down.*

Good questions, those.

About half of his entries are of little use. They ramble about seemingly irrelevant incidents: what he procured for lunch that day, for example, and an insult that was levelled at him by a rude cloth vendor, where (more interestingly) he was trying to buy silk. Silk!

Nothing we know about W suggests he was rich enough for silk garments, or of that kind of social standing either. The man seems to have come into some money and was blowing it in fine style. Surmising that his pursuit of the grave might not have been spontaneous. Somebody paid him. Theft of Bill no coincidence, perhaps. Was he keeping records to satisfy whoever was bankrolling his quest?

He hated Lavenham. Noisy, crowded and without beauty, he says. But he had no thoughts of going elsewhere; too convinced that D's grave must be somewhere nearby. Guessing that his rough map shows some part of the town, though comparing it to contemporary maps of the place has not yet yielded anything. Little indication of where he got the map, though he does say he paid a grave-digger ten shillings for information.

Ten shillings! That was a lot, for the time.

Journal ends abruptly, said Val's final message. *Seemed to think he was near to finding the grave, though did not give further details. Off he went in a spirit of high expectation, and... who knows. Did he find the grave, but for some reason abandon the journal? Did something happen to him? Cannot discover. No reference to a John Wester anywhere that seems relevant.*

As I read this last message, a final one popped up saying simply: *Nor Drogryre either.*

'Zareen,' I said. 'We are in dire need of your macabre mystery-solving skills.'

Zareen smirked. 'What is my quest?'

I thought. There were lists of outstanding questions here, but I couldn't reasonably dump them all on Zareen. What did we most want to know?

'Drogryre,' I decided. 'There is something about her that doesn't add up. Why is there no record of her? We know of many powerful witches and sorcerers from the time; why not her?'

'There must be something, somewhere,' said Zareen, already reaching for her tab. 'Something's put the wind up our friends at Ancestria Magicka, anyway.'

'Exactly. They've found something that we haven't, perhaps because they're looking in different places.'

Zareen frowned, thoughtful. 'I wonder if she was a sorceress,' she mused.

'What?'

'Well. We prize *some* magickal history, but there are parts we would prefer to forget. Or if not to forget, exactly, then we at least refrain from honouring those kinds of practitioners. Think black magick, Ves. Simplistic term, I know, but it's your necromancers, your wicked witches, your demon-summoning gutter-dwellers... those kinds of people.' Zareen maintained this narration without looking at me, her fingers flickering over her screen. 'Real life as we know it is full of shining characters, of great deeds, grand powers and magnificent achievements... course, it's also full of shit, and history is no different. But nobody wants to turn over the rocks and look at the shitty stuff.'

'Except you,' I said.

Zareen's smile flashed. 'Except for me. You need a strong stomach for it, sometimes, but there's some interesting stuff down there. And I happen to think it is important to know the worst of one's past as well as the best. Now, here's something interesting.' She passed her tab to me.

She had found an entry from somebody's blog, dated 2012. *Lavenham's Secret History of Witchcraft,* read the title.

I skimmed through the post (it was long). Written, I had no trouble guessing, by a non-magicker, it nonetheless contained some promising hints: *Did you know that the quaint, quirky town of Lavenham was once the site of some of the most horrific witch trials of the 1600s?*

'They had a coven?' I said, blinking. 'Huh.' I shouldn't have been surprised, really. Lavenham might be a small, nothing-much place now, but back in Drogryre's time it was a bustling merchant town. It wasn't that unlikely for a coven to put down roots there.

Zareen retrieved her tab. 'By the looks of it, more than one, and not just the shiny kind either.'

'You mean they had one of *those* kinds of covens?'

'Ohh, yes. The town's supposed to have declined a long way by the seventeenth, so if they had that much activity still going on even then, I'd be willing to bet it was quite the happenin' scene a century or two earlier.'

Magickers only form covens when they want to do something really difficult, something requiring the pooling of a lot of magickal power. Sometimes people do it for good, noble reasons; lots of covens were formed to battle the Sweat, for example. Lavenham might well have had one or two of those.

But as with all areas of human endeavour, some covens were (or are) formed for slightly less heroic reasons, too. Like, just for instance... 'Raising the dead?' I suggested.

Zareen grinned. 'Oh, I *hope* so.'

14

'Undead sorceresses,' I said. 'Lovely.'

'I love you,' said Zareen.

I blinked. 'Thank you. Er, why?'

'It's been an *age* since I last had a good corpse-raising mystery to sink my teeth into.'

I winced a bit inside. The near juxtaposition of *corpse* and *teeth-sinking* was doing unfortunate things to my brain. 'Thank you for those mental images.'

'Always welcome, my darling.'

'You really are pleased with me, aren't you?'

She beamed at me.

'Then you should be pleased with Jay, too. He got the book.'

Her smiled faded. 'So, new questions. I cannot yet say whether Drogryre was involved with any of these covens, or if so, which type. But somebody really wanted to find her grave, and I'd say it's an awfully big coincidence that the area happens to have a history of necromancy as well.'

'Bill said Wester expected to find some kind of treasure.'

'He might have been promised something by way of a reward, if he was successful. Or they might have guaranteed his interest by telling him there were riches to be uncovered.'

'So you don't think there was treasure?'

'From what you've told me, Bill dismissed the idea, and he ought to know. That said...' Zareen sat back again. 'There was sometimes a tradition for magickers being buried with things like their grimoires, their Wands, their familiars (mummified), or any other personal artefacts they possessed some strong connection to. But I think Bill would have known about things like that.'

'Bill *was* her grimoire.'

'Eventually. I doubt she pulled Bill out of her hat the moment she took up magick. He's the kind of accomplishment that crowns a lifetime career, and presumably she had some other, more ordinary grimoire throughout her life up to that point. Even if she did, though, it's unlikely either Wester or Ancestria Magicka had any interest in that. Bill ought to have been enough.'

'So no treasure, no grimoire, probably no artefacts.'

'I'm telling you! It has to be necromancy.'

'Maybe back then, but now? The woman's been nothing but bone for centuries. What could anybody hope to accomplish with the skeleton of a long-dead sorceress? If they want to raise a strong magicker from the dead, how about somebody, er, fresher?'

That gave Zareen pause. 'It is harder with the recently deceased,' she said, though with a little doubt. 'People keep track of corpses nowadays. Nobody dies of plague and gets chucked into mass graves anymore. It's one thing to go dig in a field somewhere for somebody long-forgotten; quite another to crash an active graveyard and walk off with someone's grandmother.'

'Still, though,' I persisted. 'When you raise a magicker from the dead, what's the intent?'

'Enslavement to your will.'

'Right — as an undead being still capable of practicing magick, in some form or another. You want to purloin their abilities for your own use, which is why deceased Waymasters tend to have a round-the-clock guard posted over their graves for about six months straight. If this is the goal, do you think a crumbling old skeleton would be of any interest to anybody?'

Zareen frowned. 'I feel like I know the answer to this, but it's not coming to mind.'

'The answer?'

Zareen lunged for her tab again, and then wandered off to feverishly scan her bookshelves. 'There's something about skeletons,' she muttered. 'I once read about a spate of grave-robbings — fifty years or so ago now — that puzzled everyone at the time for the same reasons you've just come up with. The graves that were targeted were all the resting places of magickers, and all ancient. None of the disinterred were under three hundred years dead. What would anybody want with a crop of crumbling old bones, as you put it? I don't remember now if that mystery was ever solved, *but,* there was another case in the late Victorian era where someone went so far as to advertise. Advertise! Some chap was paying well for the bones of magickers, with a fat bonus offered for a complete skeleton. He was shut down pretty quickly, and no record remains as to what he wanted to do with the bones.' Zareen wandered from shelf to shelf as she spoke, occasionally tapping at her tab. I realised I had entirely lost her attention, and stood up.

'Let me know what you dig up,' I said.

Zareen grinned, not too lost in thought to appreciate my execrable pun. 'Will do.'

My phone buzzed as I stepped out into the corridor. Jay calling.

'Can I borrow Bill?' I said without preamble.

A slight pause. 'By "borrow", do you secretly mean "elope with to the border"?'

'No.'

'Then yes. But quickly, we're leaving for Lavenham any minute.'

'We are? What for?'

'Drogryre's grave.'

'You found something!'

'Not as such. It occurred to Milady that Amelia will notice her notebook missing as soon as she wakes up — which probably happened about an hour and a half ago — and she and her esteemed colleagues will probably speed up the timetable on whatever they are doing accordingly. Ergo, she would like us on the scene.'

'Genius.' Why bother figuring out the site of the grave ourselves, if we could just let them do it and then follow? 'Provided we can find them, of course.'

'I put my tracker on Mercer.'

'You... you did? When?'

'In the middle of that fist-fight you were so eager to break up.'

Ah.

To hide my embarrassment, I hastily told Jay about Zareen's theory. 'Great,' he said. 'She can do that, you and I are going to go do this.'

'Yes, sir.'

He hung up.

It had not occurred to him to mention where he was, or anything useful like that. Nor had it occurred to me to ask. So, I merely checked that I still had my Sunstone Wand within reach, and headed off to the Waypoint in the cellar.

Though I did pop back into Zareen's room first.

'Zar, we're going grave-hunting.'

She was up out of her chair like a shot. 'Don't you dare go without me!'

'Wouldn't dream of it.' I grinned.

She tried to take all seven of her books along, then regretfully bowed to practicality and set four of them back. Then another one.

'Corpse-hunting now, reading later,' I told her.

The last two went back onto the desk with a *thump*. 'There's vital information somewhere in there.'

'They will wait for you. Boots! Phone! Quickly!'

Zareen scurried about in a brief frenzy, and within moments we were both on our way downstairs.

I could have left her to read in peace, of course, and in some ways that would have been ideal; we were in need of information. But I wanted her with us for two reasons.

One: the pall of corpse-thieving, bone-harvesting, undead-raising shenanigans hanging over this business was growing thicker by the hour, and we had no one better to deal with that kind of thing than Zareen.

Two: If we went grave-robbing without her, she would literally never forgive me.

Jay took Zareen's presence with admirable grace, while Zareen took the simpler expedient of virtually ignoring him. That was all right. Better that than sniping at each other. Jay had Bill with him, and I could not contain a coo of delight as the lovely heavy tome was put into my hands. 'You have five minutes,' said Jay. 'Then put him somewhere out of sight.'

'Bill!' I said, as Jay began his preparations for departure. 'Quick! What do you know about raising the dead?'

'I can assure you!' said Bill. 'My mistress was never a friend to that sort of activity!'

'So you don't know anything?'

'Nothing at all!'

Was it my imagination, or did cool, composed Bill sound a little bit shrill?

Hmm.

Zareen said, 'How about bone-harvesting, Bill? Specifically magicker's bones.'

Bill merely said, 'How good it is to see you again, Miss Dalir.'

'Thank you,' said Zareen. 'That's lovely.'

'I am rather lovely,' said Bill.

'Utterly. Now answer the question.'

Bill gave a bookish sigh, and shuffled his pages. 'I am no expert, you understand...'

'We understand completely.'

'...but my mistress did have one or two bone talismans in her possession at the time of her death.'

'Talismans?' said Zareen. 'What were they for?'

'They held unusual protective powers, usually along similar lines to their original owners' abilities.'

'So if I died, someone could use my bones to protect against curses?'

'If you possess a talent for hexes, Miss Dalir, then yes.'

Zareen shrugged this away, unimpressed.

'Superstition?' I asked her in an undertone.

'Sounds like it to me. Codswallop.'

We weren't getting very far with Bill, and Jay's whirling Winds were beginning to whirl in earnest. I raised my voice to be heard over the noise and half-shouted, 'What about a complete skeleton, Bill? What if somebody got hold of every bone in Zareen's body?'

Bill went very quiet.

'Bill!'

'Miss Vesper,' he finally said. 'Miss Dalir. I hold you both in the very highest esteem, and therefore permit me to advise you never to allow yourselves to be caught up in anything of that nature.'

'Why? What does it do?'

'And should you happen to die in untoward circumstances, I hope you will ensure that your loved ones will keep your remains safe from any such interference.'

Zareen's eyes may have lit up at the words *untoward circumstances,* but I felt confused — and slightly alarmed. Bill was serious, very serious. 'Why, Bill?' I tried again.

But Bill would say no more.

'Put the book away, Ves!' Jay ordered, and I obeyed, because to drop Bill somewhere in between here and East Anglia would be more than my job's worth.

And away we went.

I could not decide whether I was more relieved or disgusted by Zareen's manner of handling the journey, for she was untouched by it. We emerged inside a circle of sapling birches in the midst of a tiny copse, and Zareen strolled into the adjacent wheat field not only with perfect composure but actually with a great yawn, as though the whole process was on the duller side of human endeavour.

Jay and I exchanged a look of mutual aggravation, and I am certain we shared a mutual resolve to show no sign of discomfort whatsoever.

Said copse proved to be in between two great, rolling fields, and on the not-too-distant horizon was a town. 'Is that Lavenham?' I asked Jay.

'Well,' he said with a tiny smile. 'I hope so.'

'Are they here yet?'

Jay shook his head.

'Onward!' said Zareen, smiling in the evening sunshine as the spring breezes ruffled her glossy black hair. She took off for Lavenham at an easy, loping run, looking like an advert for washing powder, or possibly for hair care products.

'She doesn't get out of the study much,' I said to Jay by way of apology.

He grunted.

Lavenham, to my delight, was roaring drunk. The buildings looked as though it had been raining brandy for the past two hundred years and they couldn't stop giggling. Crooked, timber-framed, oddly-coloured old things, they wobbled and swayed and leaned against each other for support. Next to this wild display of character, the newer constructs looked drab and featureless. It wasn't difficult to find our way to the oldest parts of the town, where Drogryre's grave must be. We bought chips from a tiny chip shop and hastily devoured them on our way through the narrow streets, eyes everywhere at once, yet with no idea what we were looking for. I suppose we thought something obvious would pop out at us when we walked past it; that we'd know it when we saw it.

Well, it didn't.

'So,' I said after a while, when we had walked past the same perpendicular-gothic church twice over. We had checked the graveyard, just in case there happened to be a stone conveniently engraved with "Here lies Drogryre, sorceress and possible necromancer, 1485." There was not. 'If you were a fifteenth-century grave digger, where would you say is the most obvious place to bury a plague victim?'

'Or several,' said Zareen.

Or several. How were we going to pick Drogryre's individual skeleton out of a whole pile of bones? A problem to deal with... later.

'Church graveyards would fill up pretty quickly,' said Zareen. 'They'd be buried in a plague pit.' She had her phone out as she said this and was furiously typing something.

'Somewhere out beyond the edges of the town,' added Jay. 'I wouldn't bury plague-ridden corpses in my back garden.'

'Good point.' We needed to avoid the old town, then. What was empty land a few hundred years ago had probably been developed with new buildings somewhere in the last century or so, and these were spread out around Lavenham in every direction. Where to go?

'That way,' said Zareen after a minute, and pointed in what seemed to me to be a random direction.

'What?'

'This way.' Zareen set off, waving her phone at us. 'A probable plague pit was discovered in 1963 when the foundations were being dug for a new building.'

'They built a new house over a pitfull of plague victims?' Revolted, I hurried after Zareen.

'No, they built the house somewhere else.'

Jay said: 'Er, how did you find this out?'

A fair question. I had conducted a thorough search for information about the town and its environs, too, and come up with very little on the topic.

'Database,' said Zareen unhelpfully.

'What?'

'I have access to a database for this kind of stuff.'

'Plague pits?!'

'Plague pits, burial sites of unusual significance, haunted houses. Mostly with some link to magick somewhere along the line, but not always.' She turned to flash a brilliant smile in Jay's direction, thoroughly aware of how appalled he was. 'That kind of stuff.'

Jay walked in silence for a moment. 'I don't know whether to be more aghast that such a thing exists, or that you take such obvious delight in it.'

'This is why I brought Zareen,' I told him. 'She's vital to our quest.'

Jay muttered something I could not hear.

We trawled all the way to the other side of the town again, and at length arrived at... a car park.

'Hm.' Zareen frowned. 'I didn't notice anything about it being paved over.'

I stamped a foot on the smooth tarmac. It yielded not one whit.

Jay coughed. It sounded suspiciously like a strangled laugh.

'It is of no consequence,' said Bill suddenly from inside my bag. 'My mistress is not here.'

15

I FUMBLED THE BAG open and dragged Bill out. 'What do you mean, she isn't here?'

'She is not here. I detect no trace of her presence.'

'Bill, she's been dead for more than five hundred years. There is nothing left of her to detect.'

'That is not necessarily true. A strong bond was formed between us, and I would know if she was nearby.'

Damn it. 'I take it you haven't sensed any trace of her presence anywhere else?'

'I am afraid not.'

'Not even at the churchyard?'

'No.'

I felt, for one awful moment, like hurling Bill into the nearest of the puddles left by last night's rain. I contained the impulse. It wasn't his fault that we were apparently barking up the wrong tree.

'Any sign of *them*?' I asked Jay.

He shook his head. 'Nowhere near here.'

I began to get a bad feeling. 'Bill. Are you certain your mistress died here?'

'Perfectly.'

'I hate to be insensitive, but truly? You... did you see her die?'

Bill hesitated. 'Well, no.'

Damn it.

'She became very ill indeed, and with such speed that her imminent demise was inevitable. Soon afterwards, she... well, she never came back for me again, and some little time later the contents of her house were removed, including me.'

'Maybe she didn't die.'

'But.' Bill's voice developed a forlorn quality. 'Why then did she never return for me?'

'Good question.'

'Call Val,' said Jay.

My thought, too, but it was not necessary. My phone began to buzz at that moment, and it was Val calling. I put her on speaker.

'Yes!' she said. 'We have all been a bunch of idiots, and I thought you would like to know.'

'You mean our favourite plague-ridden sorceress didn't die in Lavenham?'

'So you figured that out.'

'Only just.'

'How?'

'Well, we're in Lavenham and she isn't.'

Val snorted. 'Zareen's idea interested me, so I went looking in some other, less accessible places—'

'Which ones?' I said quickly. If you catch Val off guard, she will occasionally let something slip.

Not this time. 'Let's just call them the dark depths of forbidden knowledge and leave it at that. Anyway, there is no record whatsoever of any sorceress, witch or other magicker anywhere in Suffolk of the name of Drogryre. Not five hundred years ago, and not ever.'

'Oh.'

'There is, however, quite a lot about a major sorceress called Diota *Greyer*, commonly called Dio.'

This time, it was my own self I felt like hurling into a puddle. Dio Greyer. I had seen for myself that Wester's handwriting was terrible, and Val had told me that his spelling and punctuation were decidedly eccentric. Why had it not occurred to me that we might have interpreted her name wrongly? And for that matter... 'Why didn't we stumble over her before?' I asked Val.

'Because she's not the type of sorceress we like to remember. She was the High Witch of Lavenham's black coven until 1485 when she suddenly disappeared. Serious necromancy, Ves, the really nasty stuff.'

'Bill's absolutely certain she was very ill.'

'She might well have caught the Sweat, but not everyone died of it. Or it might have been something else, like a hex. This is an era when people lived in daily terror of demons and evil spirits, after all. Remember Wharram Percy? Graves stuffed with decapitated corpses? People believed the dead could come back and attack the living, partly thanks to the activities of people like Dio Greyer. And they were terrified enough of this to mutilate and burn their recently deceased in order to prevent it. She would not have been popular, if her neighbours discovered what she was doing.'

That raised some interesting possibilities. 'Do you think that was why people were looking for her grave? To burn her bones, so she couldn't come back?'

'Maybe. Doesn't explain Ancestria Magicka's interest in her now, though.'

'Harvesting the bones as talismans? Protection against undeath, or the undead?'

'Maybe, but it seems a bit far-fetched. There are plenty of easier ways to accomplish that.'

'What about Wester?'

'Wester. Well. Either he gave up, or he, too, figured out she wasn't in Lavenham and followed her trail somewhere else — leaving Bill behind, for some reason.'

'Where does her trail go, Val?'

'Brace yourself.'

'Braced.'

'Right. There aren't any more recorded references to a Dio Greyer after 1485, so at first I was still inclined to think she'd died that year. But! A few years later, there was a kerfuffle at a town only about fourteen miles from Lavenham when a conspiracy was uncovered. Somebody called Edyth Grey (and coven) was brought in to resurrect a recently-deceased earl and restore him to power instead of his son, who was unpopular. A couple of years after that, an alderman was witnessed to have died suddenly one night when he choked on a bone at dinner — only to reappear the next morning, in poor health but apparently alive. He "lived" for another week, during which time he completed some important business which was very much in the interests of the masters of a local wool guild. There are half a dozen more stories like this one across Suffolk, all within an approximately ten-year period.'

'So Dio Greyer survived the Sweat (or her dose of hexing), fled Lavenham in a hurry on pain of decapitation and burning, and became a freelance necromancer-for-hire elsewhere.'

'Looks like it.'

'I think I'm going to like her,' said Zareen.

'Undoubtedly. In case you're interested, Edyth (or Edita) Grey died in 1496 at Bury St. Edmunds.'

'Of?'

'Hanging.'

I felt a chill at those words, and Bill's earlier warning floated back through my mind. If death-by-hanging did not qualify as *untoward circumstances,* what could? 'You're certain?'

'Yes. Unfortunately, so's Ancestria Magicka. Amelia's notebook mentions "Bury", which threw me off for a while because there's a town in the Manchester area with that name. But it's common shorthand for Bury St. Edmunds, too.'

'Val, you are a miracle.'

'I know.'

'Bury St. Edmunds?' said Zareen when I'd hung up. She had an arrested look, and her mind was obviously somewhere else.

'Does that ring some bells?'

'Maybe.' She disappeared into her phone.

'There's a bus,' said Jay. 'Leaves from the Swan in ten minutes. Half an hour's ride.'

'Where's the Swan?'

'We passed it twice an hour ago, but... no, never mind. This way. We can make it if we run.'

We ran.

'THEY'RE HERE,' SAID JAY the moment we got off the bus in the centre of Bury St. Edmunds.

'Where exactly?' I asked.

'Look, I don't know what Indira and Orlando did to these things to get so specific a reading on my position at Ashdown, but I can't replicate it. You've used these things, Ves.'

'Not much, actually. I rarely lose things.'

Jay looked faintly abashed. 'Oh. Well, they work best within a fairly short range. The closer you are to the tracker-bead, the more accurately you'll be able to pinpoint its location.'

'Oh! A warmer-warmer-warmest type thing.'

'Exactly. We aren't close enough to Mercer right now to pin him down to a street or whatever, but he's within probably about ten miles of us.'

'You should ask Indira what they did. It might be useful to know.'

'She probably wouldn't tell me. Keeping secrets is the only way she can one-up me, most of the time.' He stuck his hands into the pockets of his favourite dark leather jacket — now happily restored to him — and looked around. 'So, where did they bury hanged corpses five hundred years ago?'

'Forget it,' said Zareen.

'What?'

'Forget where they buried anybody. She isn't there.' She spoke with a kind of suppressed excitement, and her eyes were shining. 'Who's up for a ghost hunt?'

Jay looked uncertain, as well he might. It was almost eight o' clock, and the sun was sinking into the horizon. 'Explain?' he said.

'What do you two know about haunted houses?'

'Sod all,' said Jay.

'Same,' said I. 'Is there much to know?'

Zareen rolled her eyes. 'All right, my sceptical friends. Most so-called haunted houses aren't haunted at all, I grant you that much, and many that are can boast no more than an occasional flicker of spirit activity. But this is not the whole story. Scattered across our beloved country are a handful of seriously, properly haunted buildings. They could more accurately be termed *possessed*, in fact. This rarely happens by accident, and it's difficult to arrange.'

'We're a bit pressed for time, Zareen,' said Jay.

'I *know*. This is important.'

'Okay, sorry.'

Zareen took a deep breath. 'A spirit is more likely to linger after death if they died suddenly, or at a time when it seemed particularly important to them to be alive for a while longer. If you want to harness such a spirit for something like this, it's customary to bury the body under the floor of a house, or better yet in the walls themselves. Then, through use of a few charms and spells which (I need hardly add) are horribly illegal these days, you can bind the poor soul to the house itself.'

'Why would you want to?' I asked.

'It makes for a kind of bastardised version of *our* House. Doors that open and close by themselves, hopefully when you want them to. Lights which switch on and off as required, temperature regulation, immediate repulsion of anybody you don't want stepping over the threshold. Et cetera. The more powerful the spirit and the better the binding, the more interesting the options.'

It turned my stomach to imagine such a practice in anything like the same context as our beloved House. Magickal slavery of a tormented spirit wasn't something I wanted to connect with my Home, or with Milady. But I put the idea out of my head; something to think about later. 'All right, so... you think this is what's become of Greyer?'

'Her last known place of residence prior to her execution was at the end of Maynewater Lane. About a year after her death, people began to say that the house was haunted. The residents fled, and it was taken instead by one Maud Grey, who lived there in spite of its haunting for twelve years before the house mysteriously disappeared.'

'A *house* disappeared?' said Jay incredulously.

'Well,' Zareen amended. 'It was only a small one. A cottage, really. It reappeared here and there for the next couple of decades before vanishing for good, and eventually a new house was built on the spot. And look.' Zareen held out her phone. On the screen was a picture of an old, hand-inked map of the town in the fifteenth century; she had zoomed in over Maynewater Lane. 'Can we have Bill a sec?'

I saw her point at once. I hauled Bill out of his bag and opened him up to the page with Wester's crude map. The lines obviously correlated with those of the map Zareen had found, and my heart leapt with excitement. 'The X is where her house used to be?'

'Yep!'

'Hey, we've found her. Good job.'

Zareen beamed at me.

'Maud Grey,' Jay mused. 'Family?'

'Probably a sister.'

Jay nodded. 'So we've found her, but on the other hand... er, any idea where the house went to?'

'Well, there are scattered accounts over the next few hundred years of people sighting cottages or even entire mansions which vanish into the mist, or which simply aren't there when they come back. There appear to be three such stories that match up.' She checked her screen. '1572. A timber-framed cottage was spotted by a farmer on Tut Hill, but a day later it was gone. 1678, the sister of the local vicar saw a cottage fade into the mist in much the same spot. And in 1737, a tradesman's wife was held up on the road outside a ramshackle cottage in the same parish. The highwayman went in and the carriage rolled on, but the next day the cottage was gone and the robber was never found.'

'On to Tut Hill!' I said. 'Um, where is it?'

Zareen smiled at me. 'It's close.'

'Quickly,' said Jay. 'Because unless my trackers are talking rubbish, we're likely to be beaten to it.'

16

Tut Hill proved to be a long, long road clambering gently up an incline. It ran from Bury St. Edmunds out to a village called Fornham something, and it was mostly house-free. Only once we got as far as the village did we begin to see low stone walls and a smattering of properties set a little way back from the road.

It would have been nice if we had arrived to find a crumbling old cottage conveniently glowing in the dark, or overflowing with angry spirits, or something of the kind. But the houses there were mere ordinary brick structures, varied in style and age, all looking perfectly innocuous in the low light of late evening. A few had lights shining in the windows.

'What a fine vision of peace,' murmured Zareen approvingly.

I felt somewhat crestfallen. 'Either the cottage is very well camouflaged,' I suggested, 'or it is not here.'

'Could be either,' said Zareen cheerfully. Checking her maps, she pointed back the way we had come. 'I don't think any of the sightings ever came up this far. We've overshot the mark.'

My feet were hurting by then, for we had been trekking a while, and for a moment I felt like applying a heavy object to the general area of Zareen's head. I swallowed these unworthy feelings, and turned about, dragging Bill out of my bag as I did so. 'Bill,' I said gravely, 'we are in dire need of your assistance.'

'How may I be of use, Miss Vesper?'

He sounded sleepy. 'You weren't dozing, were you?'

'No! I have been fully alert since our last conversation! I assure you, I have not missed a single—' He stopped, and if a book could be said to grow *tense*, well, Bill was about as relaxed as a block of concrete just then. 'My mistress!' he said, in a proper hollow gasp, like he was in a highly dramatic stage play.

'See. I was hoping you might say something like that.' I held him out before me as we trudged a ways back down the hill. 'Lead the way, Mister Bill, if you please.'

Bill was off like a shot, dragging me behind him like he was an overexcited terrier and I the mere human appendage on the other end of the lead.

We plunged through a gap in the blackthorn hedge, and into the field beyond. Near enough pitch dark by then, and free of the lights of any nearby houses, there was little to see by; I had to trust to Bill's good sense (did he have any?) and hope he did not lead the three of us into a pit or something. Stumbling over uneven ground, we ventured perhaps a hundred metres into the field — and then stopped.

'She is close,' hissed Bill.

I still saw no house. 'Um, you sure?'

A spectral head flickered into view not two feet from my face, and my heart gave the kind of lurching shudder people sometimes die of. 'What's yer business wit' the Grey house?' it said, teeth clattering. It had hair but no skin, and great hollow eye sockets.

'Social visit,' said Zareen coolly.

There came a sudden rushing noise, as of the displacement of an awful lot of air. It was attended by a distant, high-pitched screaming which grew rapidly closer, and then there was the shadowy bulk of a cottage looming directly before us. It screamed wordless fury in a woman's voice, and Bill flinched in my hands.

'Say no more,' I muttered.

'Hello, Mistress,' said Bill weakly.

The screaming stopped.

The front door opened, and an eerie glow emanated from within.

'Right then,' I said, and stepped forward, Jay at my elbow.

Zareen flung out an arm, halting us both before we'd gone more than a pace or two. '*Please*,' she said witheringly. 'If this doesn't qualify as Toil and Trouble, I'll eat my skulls.'

'Thank you for that mental image.'

'You're welcome.' Zareen sauntered off in the direction of the beckoning door, and Jay and I fell in step behind her.

'Where are they?' I whispered to Jay.

'Gaining on us. We have, maybe, ten minutes.'

'Excellent.'

'Excellent?' It was too dark to see Jay giving me the side-eye, but I could feel it. 'You're hatching plots, aren't you?'

'Jay. *Always*.'

'Right.'

Zareen stopped in front of the door, and gave her Society symbol. We all have the three-crossed-wands part, that's the Society bit. Mine has a winged unicorn superimposed over them. Zareen's turned out to have a skull added on. Not quite human; the eyes were too big, and it had horns.

'Er,' said Jay.

'Don't ask,' I said hastily. 'Never ask.'

'Dio Greyer?' Zareen was saying. 'Maud Grey? We are here from the Society for Magickal Heritage to—'

'—warn you of a dire plot against you,' I interposed. 'Formulated by a vile organisation calling themselves Ancestria Magicka.'

'Er,' said Jay and Zareen as one.

There was a tense silence, and then the door yawned wider. Zareen rolled her eyes at me as she went in.

'You managed to use the words "vile" and "dire" in the same sentence,' muttered Jay as he followed. 'Nice work.'

'There's much to be said for drama.' Jay, sadly, beat me to the door, so I contented myself with bringing up the rear.

The interior was a low-ceilinged, white-washed, scrupulously neat little cottage, with all the leaning door frames, exposed beams and stone floors one would expect of the period. Some things were unusual, though — like the lumpy stonework just inside the door behind which Dio Greyer's bones were presumably interred, considering the way Bill instantly plastered himself to it.

'Bill,' I hissed. 'You're hugging a wall.'

'Communing with my creator,' Bill replied, rather muffled.

Considering the kind of company I was in just then, I refrained from pointing out that Bill's creator was deservedly hanged for some decidedly questionable behaviour. I suppose it's like continuing to love your parents, even if they turn out to be psychos. The argument usually runs along the lines of "Well, I only have one mother/father/creator/whatever," as if that's reason enough all by itself. Apparently, for Bill, it was.

Then again, I had no actual proof that Bill's endearing gesture was voluntary. I certainly found it impossible to peel him *off* the wall again, when I tried.

Hmm.

'My codex!' said Dio Greyer's voice. 'Thou has't returned!'

'Well...' I demurred, redoubling my efforts to retrieve Bill. 'We had not exactly intended to—'

I stopped, because she was not listening to me. The floor shook, and the walls howled: 'Hear that, wretch! Five hundr'd years to right thy miserable failings!'

Somebody replied, a somebody with the baritone rumble of a large man. But he, I was guessing, was probably as corporeal as Dio Greyer by this time, for those tones came out of thin air, and seemed to emanate from everywhere at once. 'Beef-witted churls!' he snarled. 'Have I not faithfully served thee these five centuries and more? What use these gudgeons?'

'Gudgeons they may be, but they have brought my codex,' purred Dio. 'Which is more than I can say for *thee.*'

'Had thou not made a puppet of me, I would have done all that and more! But thou must be jaunting hither and thither, and ever on! Have me hauling thy stone and bones and plaster about like turnips, because thou didst *require* it, and never a day's rest!' The walls shuddered, and the floor trembled so hard I almost lost my footing. Stones rumbled, plaster flaked, and somewhere at the back of my mind Dio Greyer was screaming again.

'Er,' I intervened. 'Mr. Wester?'

There came a shocked silence. Then: 'How didst thou come by my name?'

'It's in the book,' I said, apologetically. 'Why did you sell it?'

And there I'd made a mistake. '*Sold?*' shrieked Dio Greyer, at such a pitch as to shatter my ears. 'SOLD! Lying wretch! Thieving lily-liver! Didst thou not have courage enough to speak truth to thy mistress!'

'Thou didst slay me anyway,' rejoined Wester. 'I ought to have spoken truth to thee, were it all the vengeance I could win. Yes, I sold thy miserable codex! A foul-mouthed object! I was well rid of it.'

'And if it was foul-mouthed, I know at whose door to lay the fault!'

The argument went on in similar style for some time, and with such heat that the three of us were forgotten. We gathered into a protective knot (for we felt as though an earthquake raged around us, so much did the cottage rumble and sway with the force of Greyer and Wester's fury).

'So,' I said. 'Wester discovered where to find Dio, and got rid of Bill along the way — only she was not quite as dead as she was supposed to be, and he found himself slightly unpopular when he arrived. With Maud, too.'

'Understandably,' said Zareen. 'And the sisters slew him and stuffed him into the walls.'

'Not quite so understandably.'

'It was rather rude.'

'What did he mean about hauling the house around?'

Jay frowned. 'I have an idea about that.' He strode to the nearest wall and hammered upon it, ignoring, with enviable dignity, the rain of plaster-powder that fell upon his head. 'Hey!' he bellowed. 'Shut it!'

To my surprise, this worked. 'Hast thou something to share, little man?' said Dio acidly.

'A question,' Jay answered. 'For John Wester.'

'Speak,' said Wester.

'Were you a Waymaster, in life?'

'I was among the finest!'

'I suppose that explains why you were tapped to find Greyer's grave.'

'And find it, I did. Along with my own.'

'It was, what, 1508?'

'Mayhap.'

I put the pieces together then, too. Maud Grey had lived in the house for twelve years after her sister's death, and then it had vanished. Courtesy of Wester, an enslaved Waymaster. 'But there's no henge...?' I began.

'Didn't always have to be,' said Jay briefly. 'We're crap at it these days, need all the help we can get. Magickal decline, and all that.'

'So you can't haul entire houses around?'

'No.'

'I'm disappointed.'

Jay stuck out his tongue at me.

'What became of Maud?' I said, more loudly. 'Where's your sister, Dio?'

My question went unanswered, because the front door blew open and two people burst into the room. One of them promptly fell over the worn oak chair I had quietly placed directly in the way of the entrance, and went sprawling. That was Mercer.

The other, Katalin, managed to avoid sharing her colleague's fate by virtue of (apparently) greater dexterity, and instead darted around it. She was aiming for me, but she did not get far. It was as though she ran into an invisible wall, or was grabbed by a pair of invisible hands, for she came to an abrupt stop and was left straining uselessly at thin air.

'What are these?' said Dio dispassionately, as though these new visitors did not even qualify as human.

'Ancestria Magicka,' I said with a bright smile. 'Come to dig out your bones, Dio, and take you away to Ashdown Castle. Isn't that right? And John, too! You will have a fine new home, with a great deal more space to rattle around in.'

'And a much, *much* bigger building to haul about,' added Zareen silkily. 'Like turnips.'

'Lots of turnips,' I added.

Katalin stopped striving to get past Dio's obstruction, and instead bent to help George Mercer to his feet. He had cut his lip on something on his way down, and looked fiercely angry. 'You cannot know what an advantage it is to you,' she said. 'Your House, I mean. To achieve something of the same must be a primary goal of my organisation.'

'We do know it,' Zareen replied. 'And the likes of Greyer and Wester are not going to get you anything like the same effect.'

'Setting aside minor issues such as the ethics of the whole thing, or lack thereof,' I amended.

'Right. There is also that.'

'An approximation will suffice, if it must,' said Mercer.

He did not add that a teleporting castle would have its own benefits, of which we could know nothing. For all our dear House's many talents, perambulating about under its own power isn't one of them.

Wester, however, was not quite pleased with the notion. 'A *castle*?!' he bawled. 'Never! I refuse!'

'Why don't we all go and have a look?' said Katalin peaceably. 'You may find that you like Ashdown. And, Mr. Wester, you will not be unaided.'

That was interesting — and horrifying. How many dead Waymasters did they propose to dig up?

... or kill? Their eagerness to recruit Jay suddenly began to look sinister, and I found myself inching nearer to him.

The same idea had occurred to him, too, judging from the appalled look on his face.

Katalin smiled at him, rather kindly. 'Oh, no,' she said. 'Living Waymasters are much more useful.'

'Reassuring,' muttered Jay. 'Thanks.'

Wester may not approve, but to Dio, the idea of Ashdown held some appeal. 'A castle,' she purred. 'I was made to be a grand lady.'

'Weren't we all,' I said, *sotto voce.*

'I have fine manners,' she continued. 'And all the graces.'

'I do not!' bellowed Wester.

'Thou wilt keep *shut* thy mouth, John!' Dio snapped. 'And do as thou art bid!'

Whatever it was that Dio did to give emphasis to her words, it could not be felt by the living save, perhaps, as a waft of freezing wind that raised the goosebumps on my skin. But that it hurt the dead was indubitable, for Wester gave a great, tearing scream, and began to babble helplessly.

'To Ashdown,' purred Dio. 'The castle. And quickly, my John.'

17

A LONG-DEAD, TORMENTED AND frightened Waymaster proved not to be the best or safest of pilots. We departed Tut Hill with a sickening lurch, and a rumbling shudder which sent everyone in the room crashing to the floor. We came down some interminable time later with an un-promising *crunch*. For a little while I lay inert, my every muscle aching and my poor head spinning dizzily.

Then Jay was at my side. 'Hup,' he said, and mercilessly hauled me to my feet. 'Steady?'

I was, just about. Shaking knees aside.

Zareen was already vertical, and on her way to the door at a bouncing trot. Katalin and Mercer were on the far side of the bare little room, looking (to my secret relief) quite as shaken as I felt. And wary, too. Why? Had they not got what they wanted in bringing the cottage here?

Assuming we had arrived at the right place, of course. Zareen soon confirmed this, for having opened the front door a crack and peeped through, she proceeded to hurl it wide open and stomped out into the darkness beyond. 'Ashdown ahoy!' she called back.

That was when a third voice spoke. 'Ashdown,' it said, low and cracked. 'I remember that name, of my youth.' It was an old woman's voice, the tones worn and faded by the passage of many a long year.

Dio sighed. 'Go back to sleep, Maud.'

'I think I will not,' said Maud.

'Ah!' I cried. 'How nice to make your acquaintance, Maud Grey. Or is it Greyer?'

''Tis Greyer,' she allowed.

'Good. Excellent.' I looked around. 'And where might you be?'

'They buried me in the back bedchamber,' said Maud.

'Buried?' scoffed Wester. 'Walled thee up, like the devil thou art!'

'I am no devil,' said Maud, winter-dry. Then she laughed, wheezing. 'At least, no more than any Greyer.'

'Who is "they"?' I wondered aloud. 'Who walled you up?'

'My grandson,' she said, with chilling indifference. 'And granddaughter.'

Considering that Maud Greyer had herself interred the body of her own, freshly-hanged sister inside the cottage's walls, I decided I did not wish to know any more about the Greyer family.

Bill, though, had no scruples. '*Ves*,' he hissed, still stuck to the wall. 'Have a care! There is nothing but evil in that one.'

'How do you know?'

'My mistress always greatly feared her sister.'

'That is not true!' shouted Dio.

But Maud chuckled. 'It hath the right of it, thy odd creation. Thou wert always easily cowed.'

I felt a chill of foreboding. Dio Greyer, necromancer and High Witch of a powerful coven, found reason to be terrified of *Maud*? That did not bode well.

Whatever Katalin and George Mercer might know about Maud Greyer, it wasn't reassuring them either. They had gone from wary to outright alarmed at the exchange, and I heard Katalin say in a fraught whisper: '*She* was not supposed to be here!'

'Aye,' said Maud. 'They made fine work of me, did they not? Put it about that I had died of the Sweat, and into the wall I went with none the wiser.' She paused, chillingly, and added in a musing tone, 'I wonder what hath become of my descendants?'

I, for one, did not want to know.

'I would like to be rid of these confines,' continued Maud after a moment. 'These rude walls, how they chafe after five hundred years!'

'You must free me, but not her!' Dio said. Her manner was commanding, but I detected a shrill note of fear somewhere behind.

'And me,' added Wester. 'But never *her.*'

'Thou shalt not leave without me.' Maud's words emerged barely above a whisper, but with a ringing power behind them that rooted me to the spot. 'Thou shalt none of you leave without me.'

The door banged shut behind me. I could not even turn to see if Zareen had come back in; my muscles were frozen, and I could not move an inch.

'I suppose you *had* to make her angry?' said Bill venomously.

The walls rattled, and something dark and liquid began to seep through the whitewash and trickle towards the floor. 'Um,' I said, my lips numb. 'Is that... that isn't *blood*, is it?'

'Yep,' said Zareen, and walked past me into the centre of the floor. 'You'd better stop, Maud Greyer,' she said severely. 'I will stand for no more shenanigans.'

I adored Zareen just then. Not only for facing Maud Greyer and her bleeding walls without a blink, but also for using the word *shenanigans* to describe them.

How exactly she was perambulatory when Jay and I and the two Ancestria Magicka operatives remained glued to the floor, well. That was another question.

'Thou art no match for me,' crooned Maud. 'Fair potential thou dost indeed possess, but thou art but an acorn to my mighty oak.' Blood began to drip from the ceiling, too, and to my horror a crack opened in the floor and swiftly widened. Something pale, unwholesome and smoky seeped through from below.

Zareen took all of this in with narrowed eyes, and nodded. 'You might be right,' she allowed. 'Mercer!'

George Mercer's head snapped up. 'No!'

'It's necessary.'

'It's not. Do something else!'

'Like what?'

Judging from the silence, Mercer had no answer to this.

'Stop being a wimp,' Zareen ordered. 'And stop pretending. The sheep routine's getting boring.'

Mercer growled something, but he proceeded to push away from the wall he'd been leaning on, and ambled over to Zareen. This, apparently, came as much to Katalin's surprise as to mine.

'Zar?' I tried. 'What exactly is going on?'

'Don't worry,' she said briefly. 'But grit your teeth.'

'What?'

She'd linked hands with Mercer, and to my stark horror her eyes turned black. I mean, Zareen's eyes are almost black anyway, but *all the whites filled in with solid black*, too. 'Can't guarantee this won't hurt a bit,' she said.

Then the same thing happened to the eyes of George Mercer, and I shut my stupid mouth.

'Ves?' said Jay uncertainly.

'Just do as she says,' I said tightly.

Maud Greyer had figured her out, too, and she was *not* pleased. 'Betrayer!' she shrieked, losing her cool in fine style. 'How durst thou turn the Arts against me!' The floor washed over with blood, and it was bubbling and boiling; my feet began to burn. The walls shook so hard I expected the ceiling to come down at any moment and bury us all, and I could hardly hear Maud's continued vituperation over the sounds of stones, tiles and beams all rattling against one another.

Zareen raised her voice to shout over the tumult. 'Five hundred years!' she intoned in an oddly ringing voice. 'Ought to have been enough to learn some bloody manners!'

'Spare me!' shrieked Dio. 'Spare John! We will do as thou dost bid us, and never seek to do thee harm!'

'Sorry,' Zareen said flatly. 'Time's up.' Drops of blood leaked from the corners of her eyes, and from Mercer's.

And, I realised, from mine.

A sharp, fierce pulse of pure power shot through the floor and raced up the walls. It manifested itself as a sea of shadow pouring forth from Zareen and Mercer and swallowed everything in its path — me, Jay, the book, all of it. That sea burned like lava and froze like ice, and every cell in my poor abused body screamed with pain.

So did I.

Somewhere in the distance I was aware of Dio and Maud Greyer and John Wester, making a cacophonous orchestra of indignation, fury and pain. But I had other things to consider, for besides the minor inconvenience of searing agony in my every organ, there were a few structural problems developing. The ceiling was raining chunks of plaster into the pools of blood below, and there came the splintering sound of stone cracking into pieces.

'Zareen!' I bawled. 'You'll bring the roof down!'

Too late. The splintering intensified, and a great, groaning tumult heralded the imminent collapse of the cottage. I had time only to grab what little magick I could muster, tears of blood pouring from my eyes, and weave up a shield before the roof shattered into chunks and rained down upon us.

My shield, shaky and feeble, did not last long. Neither did I. I'd thrown it clumsily over Jay, Zareen, Mercer and Katalin as well as myself, and I had the satisfaction of seeing it deflect at least the first wave of falling stone. But it could not bear up under the rest; my glorious, shimmering bubble dissipated into the air, a great slab of something distressingly solid collided with my head, and I passed out.

I woke up bathed in blood.

I cannot say it is the worst thing that has ever happened to me (don't ask), but it may be imagined that I was not best pleased.

The cottage lay in rubble all over the once neatly-swept floor. Moonlight shone upon the pale face of Zareen looming above me, her eyes thankfully restored to their usual colour. 'You alive, Ves?' she was saying.

I took a breath, every second of which hurt like hell. 'I wish I wasn't.'

Her lips twitched. 'Lies.'

'Fine. I hurt, but I am relieved you didn't manage to kill us all with your freaky shit.'

'Nice work with the shield.'

'Thanks.' I sat up. Jay was leaning against the remains of a wall a few feet away, his black hair almost white with dust and a fresh bruise added to his already sumptuous collection. 'Hi,' he croaked.

'You're not dead either.'

'Nope.'

Mercer was prone, apparently still out cold. Katalin sat guard by his side, cross-legged and heedless of the sticky, congealing blood she was sitting in.

All was quiet. The silence was eerie after all the noise of the past hour or so.

'They're gone?' I said to Zareen.

She nodded once.

'Uh huh. And what was that you did, exactly?'

'Forcible exorcism.' Zareen turned away and bent to pick something out of the rubble.

'Did I know you could do that?'

Zareen didn't answer.

'Zar. Are you a necromancer?' I looked sharply at Mercer. 'And him, too?'

Zareen gave me a long, measuring look, and for a second her eyes flickered once more into deep, black pools. 'Toil and trouble, remember?' she said, and her voice was as bone-dry as Maud Greyer's.

'Does that mean yes?'

'It means, don't ask.' Before I could speak again, she handed me her find — a book.

The book.

'Oh, Bill,' I sighed, stricken. 'I'm so sorry.'

'It would be ungenerous of me to reproach the heroine of the hour,' said Bill.

I didn't think so. It had not occurred to me to include Bill in my shield, and as a consequence he had been sadly crushed. He now sported three dents in his formerly pristine covers, and some of his pages were torn.

'Zareen's the heroine of the hour,' I said. 'Does it hurt?' I tried to smooth his pages as best I could, a useless gesture.

'I do not possess nerves, Miss Vesper.'

I winced, my own agonies not yet forgotten. 'That sounds nice.'

'It has its moments.'

'What is that noise?' said Jay, and hauled himself to his feet.

'What noise—' I began, but then I heard it: a thin, high-pitched whimpering coming from somewhere nearby.

Walking like an old, old man, Jay limped off into what remained of the next room. There were only the two rooms to the cottage, apparently, and the one we were in was by far the largest. Following Jay, I found what had probably once been the back bedchamber where Maud's remains were interred. It was as empty of furniture as the other room, boasting only a dusty (and now broken) chair. The floor was thick with blood, rubble and debris, but in the wan moonlight that filtered through the empty window-frame I discerned a glimpse of something incongruously brightly coloured.

The whimpering gained in volume.

'There's an animal,' said Jay, and ventured towards the window, stepping through the fallen stones with unusual care. He crouched, and began to pull away the wreckage from the corner.

A flash of pale, yellowish fur emerged, and Jay scooped up something tiny enough to fit into one cupped hand.

'Here,' he said, turning, and offered it to me.

I took it with infinite care, for it was a tiny, delicate creature, probably only recently born, and obviously in distress. It resembled a puppy, except its nose was much larger than that of a typical dog, and its forehead bore the tiny nub of a horn. I suspected, moreover, that when cleaned up and viewed in daylight, its fur would prove to be not so much yellowish as bright, sunny gold.

It was hungry, I concluded, for it seemed intent upon devouring my thumb. Fortunately, it had not yet developed much in the way of teeth.

'Ouch,' I said anyway, wincing a bit.

Jay smiled. 'I think you are the properest person to take care of a tiny fluffy thing, don't you?'

I beamed at him. 'Without doubt. But how did it come to be here?' I made to step past him to investigate the spot in the corner, but Jay got in front of me.

'I wouldn't,' he said.

'Why not?'

His face turned grim. 'There were more.'

I didn't miss his use of the past tense, and my heart sank. 'How many?'

'Two more like this one.'

I tried to get past him again, but he caught me and pushed me back. 'They're dead, Ves. No sense in upsetting yourself.'

'Yes, because I'm marshmallow. You, of course, are made from solid rock.'

He just looked at me, his mouth grim and his eyes sad.

'Fine, fine,' I sighed and turned away, cradling the sole survivor of the wreck. 'Zareen's going to cry, you realise.'

'She shouldn't. They were not crushed. I would rather say they starved.'

'Right. We'd better get this one to Miranda as soon as possible.' I would have fed it on the spot if I could, but what did a baby horned puppy eat? I could offer it a whole feast of only slightly congealed blood lightly seasoned with dust, but I doubted that would serve the purpose.

In the next room, Katalin and Mercer were deep in conversation with Zareen. I watched them for a moment, eyes narrowed, for it seemed to me that Zareen and Mercer were not quite strangers. Indeed, Zar's actions of half an hour before had strongly implied that she knew more about George Mercer than we did. 'Old friends?' I said at last, when a lull offered in the conversation.

Zareen just flashed me an enigmatic look.

'I know, I know. Don't ask. We're leaving on a mercy mission,' I said, showing Zareen the puppy. 'Can you deal with all this?'

It wasn't fair to land her with that job, since by "this" I meant the wrecked cottage, the scattered bones of those who had once been interred within its walls, the sea of blood leaking all over the grounds of Ashdown Castle and, of course, the problem of the two Ancestria Magicka operatives who were still hanging around. But Zareen is equal to anything.

'Go!' she commanded. 'Save the tiny, defenceless thing.'

'We'll send help from Home.'

'That would be nice.'

'Where's the nearest henge?' I said, turning back to Jay.

'Assuming you don't want to break into Ashdown itself at this hour, and in this state... too far to walk.'

I nodded. 'Well then. I wonder if our Chairs are still there?'

18

Miranda was not only eager to assume charge of our find; she was electrified.

Jay and I proceeded directly to her domain once we reached Home. She is the head of our Magickal Beasts division, and presides over extensive premises in the east wing. We found her in the veterinary department, tending to the damaged wing of a black bird with an unusually long, blue beak. 'Can it wait just a second?' she said when we went in, without looking up.

'One or two, but not more.' I didn't say that lightly. Our puppy had abandoned its attempts to eat my fingers almost the moment we had stepped out of the ruined cottage, and over the journey home it had seemed to lose all energy. It (or she, I think) now lay inert in my palm, worryingly lifeless.

'Right.' Miranda gently returned her bird to a large cage near the back of the room, and set it carefully atop a padded perch inside. Then she bustled back to us. She'd had a long day of it herself, by her appearance: her white coat was streaked with bird poop, some kind of animal feed and who-knew-what-else, and her blonde hair had mostly fallen out of its usually neat ponytail. She looked tired and shadow-eyed.

I held out the puppy to her. 'Starving to death. Please help.'

Miranda took my puppy, handling her very gently. She said nothing for several seconds, examining the creature with great care. Her eyes grew rather wide. 'Ves,' she whispered at last, her voice emerging as a croak. 'Where did you find this?'

I told her.

'Hnngh,' she said, and swallowed. 'Er.'

'What?'

'This is a...' she began, then stopped. 'I mean, it *can't* be, but it is.'

'Not making sense,' I offered helpfully.

Miranda shook her head, disbelieving. 'It's a dappledok puppy. They're extinct.'

'What?'

'Dead as dodos. The last known sighting of a live one was recorded in a letter in, like, the late seventeen hundreds.'

I stared. 'Oh.'

'So!' she said. 'I'll be off moving heaven and earth to save this one's life, and later we'll talk more about where you got it. Okay?' Without waiting for an answer, she charged off, taking my tiny puppy with her.

I looked at Jay. 'You've a talent for stumbling over long-lost things, it seems.'

His smile flickered. 'We still have to figure out what to do with the last one.'

I gave a long, long sigh at that, and said: 'I'm pretty sure I know exactly what will become of poor Bill.'

Baron Alban arrived bright and early the next morning. *Too* bright and early. I had no idea how he had managed to receive Milady's summons and act upon them so fast, but I supposed he must have a Waymaster at his disposal. If he wasn't one himself.

Having developed a more than passing acquaintance with the Baron by that time, I was prepared for his probable promptness, and so he found me awake, dressed and intent upon the consumption of my second cup of tea. I was only slightly droopy, and gazed at him with bleary-eyed alertness as he wandered into my usual nook in the first floor common room.

'Ves,' he said with his broad, charming smile. 'You look like you fell under a ceiling.'

I gave him my most withering look, and swallowed a great deal more tea. 'You usually manage to be more complimentary.'

'You look gorgeous. Bruises suit you.'

I waved him to a chair, ignoring that. He looked as well turned-out as ever in a dark blue suit and white shirt, his purple tie elaborately knotted. 'Please take care of Bill,' I implored him.

One brow went up. 'Bill?'

'The book. We call him Bill.'

He inclined his head, as though this declaration made perfect sense. 'Bill will have the best care, naturally. I've hopes that our bookbinders can patch him up a bit, and he'll be safe from your friends at Ancestria Magicka.'

I shrugged at that, and set down my empty cup. 'I doubt they will care about him much longer. They've had time enough to study all his workings, and will probably produce replicas soon enough.'

'And will the Society, also?'

'I have reason to believe that Milady cleared Orlando's agenda entirely in favour of the project.'

He nodded, studying my face. 'You're sad about something.'

'I am sorry for the loss of Bill. He's the most charming book I ever met.' My leave-taking from Bill the night before had been a little painful; he had not been delighted to be separated from me either, though his vanity could not but be pleased at the prospect of becoming a prized treasure of the Troll Court. I'd heard unpromising reports of the puppy, too; Miranda could only confirm that she was still breathing, and wouldn't hazard more.

'The most charming troll you've ever met is still waiting to take you out,' said the Baron, and gave me a hopeful smile.

I couldn't help perking up a bit at that. 'How obliging of him.'

'Just say the word.' He got up, and made me a graceful bow. 'I'd love to stay, but I need to get the book back to the Court. I have an escort and everything.'

'Six ruthless bodyguards?' I peeked behind him, as though there might be a team of dreamily muscle-bound trolls waiting by the door.

'Something like that.' He winked, and gave me a tiny salute. 'Call me.'

I promised.

On his way out, he passed Jay and Indira just coming in. I was intrigued to note that none of them seemed a bit surprised to see one another. 'Good timing,' said Alban with a smile, and then he was gone.

I raised my brows at Jay, but he ignored my silent question and flopped into a chair without speaking.

I looked at Indira, who was taking a seat with more care and more grace, keeping her injured arm well away from the table. 'What was that about?' I asked.

Indira looked guiltily at Jay, and said nothing.

Jay smiled at her. 'Well, go on.'

She glanced at me, and looked quickly away again. Carefully, she bent to retrieve a soft cloth bag from the floor by her feet; I hadn't noticed her carrying it when she came in. She placed this on the table before me, and sat back.

I waited for some explanation, but nothing came. 'I'm to open the bag?'

Indira nodded.

Mystified, I peeped inside. A book lay at the bottom. It was of an ancient style (thick leather covers, vellum pages, heavy silver hinges) but it looked pristine and new. Extracting it with care, I discovered that the covers were tinted dark purple, and the front was embossed with a twelve-pointed star. It weighed less than it looked like it should.

'A book!' I said, not at all enlightened.

'Open it,' said Jay.

I obeyed.

'Madam,' said the book. 'You must allow me to tell you how ardently I admire and love you.'

'Perfect,' whispered Jay, and the book gave a rather smug rustle of its pages.

'Bill?' I choked. 'But— but the Baron just took him!'

'Bill the Second,' said Jay. 'Indira's been working on it ever since we left.'

'Well, Orlando has,' said Indira, hastily disclaiming. 'I've just been, um, helping.'

Jay shook his head slightly. 'More than that. You can't deny this is mostly your own work.'

Indira looked like she wanted very much to deny it, but couldn't truthfully do so.

'That's extremely clever of you,' I said, with total sincerity. I couldn't imagine the depth of skill required to produce such a grimoire; my talents definitely don't lie in that direction. I stroked Bill the Second's covers with faint regret (all right, more than faint), and handed him back to Indira.

She did not take him. Instead, she gave me a stricken look. 'Um, don't you want him?'

'Wha... he's for *me*?'

Indira nodded furiously.

'Am I... am I allowed?'

Indira nodded again. 'This is a, um, prototype. Orlando's working on the finished design and, well, this one's spare. Milady said it was all right.'

Jay's eyes narrowed ever so slightly, but he said nothing.

I was only too glad to gather Bill Two back into my arms and give him a tight hug. 'Thank you,' I said, beaming. 'It will be my honour to work with him.'

Indira smiled back, visibly relieved. 'I'm glad you like him,' she said, already getting out of her chair.

'Won't you have some tea?' I offered, but she was in full retreat by then, and only shook her head as she vanished out the door.

I looked at Jay, and waited.

'She made him especially for you,' he said. 'Stayed up most of the night to finish him, too.'

'Um,' I said. 'Why?'

He shrugged. 'Might be that she's savvy enough to cultivate connections amongst those who are popular at Home. Or... maybe she just likes you.'

'Likes me,' I repeated numbly. 'Right.' Indira was always polite, but she still gave me the impression that she was petrified of me.

I decided that the Patels in general were a hard-to-read bunch.

Before Jay could decide upon a reply, there came the sound of tiny claws clicking against the hard floor, and the yellow dappledok puppy came creeping around the door. Her ears were down, her tail drooped and she trudged wearily in my direction as though the distance between us were almost insurmountable.

But she was alive!

'Puppy!' I blurted, overjoyed. 'Come here!'

The moment she came within reach of the table, Jay bent to scoop her up, and handed her to me. I put her in my lap, whereupon she crawled, shivering, inside my cardigan and disappeared.

I tucked the folds of my clothes around her and sat, smiling like an idiot, until Miranda inevitably appeared. 'Ves!' she said, slightly out of breath. 'Don't hate me, but I think I've lost the puppy.'

I merely pulled aside my cardigan, displaying the ball of yellow fur. 'Winnie the Unipup is fine.'

Miranda sagged against the doorframe in relief, though she looked annoyed, too. 'Look, she shouldn't be taken out of care just now at all, but at the *very* least you need to tell me.'

'I didn't take her! She showed up at the door about four minutes ago.'

Miranda blinked. 'She found her way up here?'

'I swear. Jay, back me up.'

'Every word of Ves's is the truth,' he dutifully declared.

Miranda sighed. 'Fine. Bring her back down once an hour for milk, okay?'

I tucked my cardigan back over my unipup once more, and beamed at Miranda. 'Got it, boss.'

Also By Charlotte E. English

Modern Magick

The Road to Farringale
Toil and Trouble
The Striding Spire
The Fifth Britain
Royalty and Ruin
Music and Misadventure
The Wonders of Vale
The Heart of Hyndorin
Alchemy and Argent

The Magick of Merlin
Dancing and Disaster

House of Werth

Wyrde and Wayward
Wyrde and Wicked
Wyrde and Wild

Printed in Great Britain
by Amazon